A Sea Glass
Christmas

Books by Davis Bunn

The Miramar Bay Series
Miramar Bay

Firefly Cove

Moondust Lake

Tranquility Falls

The Cottage on Lighthouse Lane

The Emerald Tide

Shell Beach

Midnight Harbor

The Christmas Hummingbird

The Christmas Cottage

The Outer Banks Series
Fortunate Harbor

A Sea Glass Christmas

A Sea Glass Christmas

DAVIS BUNN

KENSINGTON
PUBLISHING CORP.

kensingtonbooks.com

KENSINGTON BOOKS are published by

Kensington Publishing Corp.
900 Third Avenue
New York, NY 10022

Copyright © 2025 by Davis Bunn

All Kensington titles, imprints, and distributed lines are available at special quantity discounts for bulk purchases for sales promotion, premiums, fund-raising, educational or institutional use. Special book excerpts or customized printings can also be created to fit specific needs. For details, write or phone the office of the Kensington Special Sales Manager: Kensington Publishing Corp., 900 Third Avenue, New York, NY, 10022. Attn. Special Sales Department. Phone: 1-800-221-2647.

KENSINGTON and the K with book logo Reg. U.S. Pat. & TM Off.

Library of Congress Control Number: 2025936277

ISBN: 978-1-4967-5426-4

First Kensington Hardcover Edition: October 2025

ISBN: 978-1-4967-5428-8 (ebook)

10 9 8 7 6 5 4 3 2 1

Printed in the United States of America

The authorized representative in the EU for product safety and compliance
is eucomply OU, Parnu mnt 139b-14, Apt 123
Tallinn, Berlin 11317, hello@eucompliancepartner.com

THIS BOOK IS DEDICATED TO

Pam and Elmore Alexander

And

Nancy and Greg Piner

Guiding Lights

1

Two hours before dawn, Brody dreamed of the boat. It was a natural part of his routine. The night before he launched into any new race, he dreamed the dream. It was a simple confirmation that his life was on the right track. That he was exactly where he was supposed to be.

Given everything that was currently fracturing his world, Brody might have called that ironic, entering into his happiest dream. But being asleep, he simply sighed his way into the joy.

He and his crew were far off shore, the sails well set, running with the wind. It blew strong south by east, a rare gift in early winter. Brody called this a cashmere wind, because no matter how strong it blew, there was a graceful ease to the air-bound currents. It unified the crew, this gift of warm grace, intimate as a lover's caress. But the south wind was also a fickle lass, given to wild moods and untamed moments.

Clouds bunched like so many fists to his right, which meant they were flying east, out into deep Atlantic waters. And that was very strange, because when the south wind showed her untamed side, any good skipper not under the racing clock knew it was time to head for shallow waters. And Brody was always pilot and helmsman in his dream. The best there was.

So east they ran, even though the sky darkened, and the south wind now carried a heavy burden, and the distant thunder sounded her warning note. But the crew laughed as they pushed hard under full sail, reveling in the speed and the freedom only a sailor knew. Which was the way Brody's dream always went: the nine of them so intimately joined, they might as well have been breathing as one. Even now, when the cashmere wind threatened to turn thunderous and deadly. And this was the point where Brody always woke up, fully aware of the risks and challenges involved in ocean racing. He counted it as a good way to enter a race, excited and threatened in equal measure.

This particular dream, however, proved very different indeed. One moment, he and the crew were preparing for what might strike. The next, Brody was alone.

The boat was empty, crashing through waves nearly

as tall as the sixty-foot mast. Riding up the swells, fly-ing down the next. He knew a heavy squall was in-bound and wanted to slip into his rain gear. But being alone in these swells, Brody couldn't risk using the autopilot and he didn't have time to lash the wheel.

Then the dark, fistlike clouds clenched tighter and squeezed out a torrent. Brody was struck by a solid wall of water. His vision was so limited he could no longer see the bowsprit. And he sailed alone.

He hit the electronic winches to draw in the jib and restrict the mainsail. Whether or not they actually worked, he could not see.

Then his sixty-foot mast became a lightning rod.

That had actually happened twice in his sailing ca-reer. Racing in Caribbean waters always carried this risk. The second time, they had been off Grenada. The bolt had carried such force one of the crew's hair had caught fire. But this was different.

The masthead held a finial, also known as a strike terminator. The copper rod rose a foot above the mast and drew the charge down to where it could be safely grounded. Just the same, any such strike tem-porarily deafened the crew and turned the mast into a blinding pillar of fire.

Not this time.

Lightning struck in slow motion. The bolt touched the mast and went *everywhere*, illuminating the entire boat with a brilliant fiery pattern. Every stay, the gunnels, the boat itself, all of it shimmering and shrieking with the harmonic power. Slowly, inexorably, it flowed toward Brody. Ensnaring his feet, rising up his legs, encasing his body, his arms, his neck, his face and head, and . . .

BOOM.

He woke standing by his condo's open window, drenched in sweat and gasping for a breath he feared might never come.

He departed Charlotte for Morehead City at four fifteen in the morning. Brody Reames normally considered the journey a return to heaven, or rather, as close as a man with his storied past would probably ever come. But this trip was different. And not simply because of the nightmare he was unable to shake.

The new Independence Highway usually made these journeys a pleasure. Three hundred miles through Carolina's agricultural heartland, flying south of Raleigh and Durham and the Research Triangle, all the growth and tangled traffic someone else's problem. Brody Reames had lived his entire life in North Carolina and counted it as one of life's fortunate coincidences. He was leaving for the coast five days before Christmas, supposedly heading down to check out a new oceangoing racing hull. His boss normally allowed Brody to count this as a regular day at the office.

Yet on this particular morning, all he felt was a confused dread.

Two days earlier, his mother had called with news that rocked his world. She had left her husband. She had filed for a legal separation. Divorce proceedings would begin early in the new year. When Brody had asked why and why now, his mother had replied in the same calm down-east manner that had defined her entire life.

"It's time to live life on my terms," was all Mia Reames would say.

The years spent serving as chief mate and helmsman on oceangoing racers had granted Brody the ability to shut off his emotional tap. Just slam the door shut on anything other than the task at hand. Today, however, was different. His mother's news had arrived just as the rest of his world was unraveling.

The journey took just over four hours, blasting east with all the windows down. The forecast rain never arrived, though the dreamtime lightning strike remained his constant companion. Brody entered the Morehead City morning traffic, stopped for a light, and texted his sister. Olivia responded immediately, saying she was on break and to meet her in the hospital cafeteria.

He turned off 70 and entered the Carteret County Hospital's main lot. The west wing was still under

construction, and the lot was surrounded by glisten-
ing raw earth. His sister was a skilled biotechnician
and ran one of their new labs. The hospital was
forward-thinking, a rarity down east, and had set up
a flexible arrangement to assist young mothers like
Olivia.

Olivia resembled their father, only with her, the
squarish jaw and unruly dark hair became very attractive. She also possessed a brilliant mind and energy to match, and was blunt and direct, and very
open with her opinions. Brody's earliest memory was
of her watching him sleep through the narrow slats of
his first real bed. Her intelligent gaze said clearly that
she wasn't sure he was worth keeping.

The cafeteria held two Christmas trees that blinked
a seasonal welcome. His sister was seated at a window table, where the midday light cast her features
in a Renaissance glow. She was with a visibly pregnant woman Brody vaguely recognized. The fact that
Olivia was not meeting him alone told him everything
he needed to know. Olivia was not going to let him
have a private chat about their mother's decision.
Which probably meant Olivia had known about this
for some time

Olivia rose to her feet at his approach, hugged him
tightly, and said, "Welcome home."

"It's good to see you." He dropped into the chair

beside hers. Smiled to the woman seated across from them. And did not say a word.

Standing by the entrance, Brody had thought she looked familiar. Now his sister's silence confirmed it. Olivia knew they had been together, and also knew Brody did not remember the woman's name.

He waited.

The silence might have lasted for hours, sister and brother turning the moment into just another contest. But Olivia's phone rang. She glanced at the screen and rose to her feet. "I need to take this."

When Olivia walked away, the woman seated across from him said, "Cameron."

The memories clicked into place of what for him had been a summer fling with her. She was back from college and waitressing in the dockside restaurant. Brody had been training with a new team and working at his uncle's marina. Their good times lasted until he left for the ocean trials. She had not taken his casual departure at all well. Brody said, "You're not called Cammie anymore?"

"Not in years."

"I never cared for that name."

"I remember." Her smirk resembled Olivia's. "I'm surprised you do."

"Are you here visiting someone?"

"I'm a clinical psychologist now. I work one day a

week with patients here. And their families. Crisis counseling." She patted her stomach. "Though all that's about to change."

She was a handsome woman, the vivacious young lady all tucked away beneath layers of professional intelligence. In her knowing gaze was all the reason Brody needed to say, "Do you have time for a new patient?"

The words erased Cameron's quiet smugness. "What?"

Brody had uttered the words almost without thinking. The drowning man reaching out for whatever help was there at hand. He knew an instant's utter panic, then nothing. At some visceral level, he knew this was the right thing to do. And the right time.

His silence unsettled her. "You really mean this? You want to enter therapy?"

"If you'll have me. I do. Yes."

"Brody . . . why?"

It's time, he wanted to say. But he knew that wasn't enough. "My life is about to go through some major transitions. I want to make sure I take the right steps."

The smirk was history now. She studied him with the dispassionate intelligence of a true professional. "Are you saying you want to change?"

"The change is happening whether I want it or not."

"That's not what I mean, Brody. And I think you know it." Cameron's entire focus was on him. The hospital, the cafeteria, the hand still resting on her middle, the people at neighboring tables, his sister standing in the far corner, all gone. "My question goes deeper than whatever changes are being foisted upon you from outside. I ask again. Do you want to change?"

The question resonated at gut level. "Want is too strong. But it's time."

"Is it?" She studied him a long moment. "If your mother's divorce is the reason your world's been shaken, you need to accept that Mia Reames is stronger than she appears. Stronger than either of you probably realize."

"That's not—"

"Mia will get through this all on her own. And your desire to manage change, if this is what's driving your current need, will fade." Lights blinking on the nearest Christmas tree softened her face but not her tone. "In time, you'll go back to your old ways. And you'll forget all about this conversation. Or try to."

"That's exactly what I don't want." The words and the way Cameron regarded him all hurt. Because they were precisely what he deserved. Brody felt himself perspiring, both from how she had stripped away his defenses and because he was determined now to continue. "What Mom is going through is only part of it. The spur that's pushing me to do what I've needed to face for years. It's all come together. And I need help."

Cameron remained distant, unmoved, analytical. Her voice matched her gaze. "I'm not convinced this is real."

"And I'm saying—"

"Hear me out, Brody. It's real for you *now*. But true change means months of work. Sometimes years. It requires a dedicated commitment." Even her smile carried a clinical edge. "Quite frankly, I don't see you holding this ability."

He nodded, not in agreement, but because it was what he deserved. "Just the same, I want to work with you."

She shook her head. Definite now. "I can't erase how you treated me. Or the pain you caused."

"Which is why I'm asking." Trying to keep his voice level, hide the raw, almost acidic element. "You've seen my dark side. What I need to move beyond."

He could see the response was unexpected. It shook her. Cameron remained silent until she noticed Olivia was heading back in their direction. "I can't accept you as a patient, Brody. Not yet, anyway. And perhaps not ever. Our past . . . you understand? But I am willing to speak with you as—"

He could see how she backed away from using the word *friends*. "I do understand. And thank you."

She pulled a card and pen from her jacket pocket, scribbled, passed it over. "I can speak with you this time tomorrow. Call my cell." She halted his thanks with an upraised hand. "Between now and then, I want you to think about this. What does change mean to you? At the deepest personal level, how would you define healthy personal change?"

Brody could see the dismissal in her gaze. Which was good, because he had no interest in Olivia seeing just how deeply his world had been shaken. He rose to his feet and said, "Until tomorrow."

2

Rae Alden walked the Carteret County Hospital corridor in a daze. Everything she saw felt alien. She wanted to say the faint construction odors drifting from the unfinished wing were what left her feeling nauseous, but her new office held remnants of the same smells and she was fine with that. Today, here, was different. And it all had to do with what had just taken place.

Abruptly, her legs refused to carry her. Rae settled into a hardwood bench across from the nurses' station. The woman on duty glanced up and offered a vague smile, then went back to her work. There was nothing new, or wrong, in somebody needing a moment to recover.

The doctor who had called her was a new one, at least to Rae. She knew him vaguely, mostly by reputation. Dr. Kendrick Asher had grown up in Morehead, then left, like so many others with potential. He had graduated from UNC, undergrad and medical school, and wound up staying in Chapel Hill. Then last year he had accepted a position as resident internist at Carteret.

Kendrick Asher was a couple of years older than Rae. She vaguely recalled an intelligent and handsome teen whose dark complexion and sharp features had suggested a trace of Indian blood. The only significant difference between her memories and the man she had met with today were strands of silver in his hair and his gold-rimmed spectacles. Dr. Asher had greeted her with an utter absence of warmth and dived straight in. "Our records show you are attorney of record for Emma Alden."

Rae opted to match his tone and directness both. "Why am I having this conversation with you?"

"I have been asked to supervise—"

"Where is Doc Arnold?"

"Ill."

"Then I'll wait."

"You can—your aunt may not be able to."

"I don't believe you."

He was at least capable of showing irritation. "Evidently you share your aunt's attitude towards the medical profession."

Suddenly his irritation had both a name and a reason. "Emma gave you a piece of her mind," Rae said, not bothering to hide her smile. "I bet that stung. And from what I'm observing, you probably deserved it."

He leaned back. "Rae Alden. I remember a very intense young lady who was out to conquer the world."

"And look where it got me. I remember you, too."

He might have smiled. A trace. Nothing more, and not for long. "Shall we start over?"

"I suppose we can try."

"Doc Arnold brought me along for his most recent visit. I've been back once since." Another tight smile. "A visit I won't soon forget."

"Is that normal, a hospital kind of doctor making house calls?"

"If I'm going to fit myself back into this community, some rules that work fine in other places need to be remolded to suit this region." He glanced at the computer screen. "I suggested to your aunt that she might consider hospice care."

The entire room did a sudden swoop and dive. "I'm sorry, what are you saying?"

"Her condition is deteriorating rapidly. There will soon be a point in time when the power of such decisions will be taken from her."

Rae gripped the sides of her chair, struggling to stop the room from spinning. "She's had spells for years. As long as I can remember."

"This time is different. Do you want me to go into detail?"

"No." The doctor's impersonal nature came into focus. It gave her something to grab onto. A way to draw herself back from the brink. "I've lived with Emma's health issues all my adult life."

"Then you must have known this time was coming. I requested this meeting because that time has arrived."

The doctor began describing stages she should expect to see, timing them out and suggesting the level of care that each would require. Rae forced herself to make notes, because nothing really registered. And all of this was important. Whether she wanted or could handle the prospect did not matter. Emma's care and comfort was all that mattered, all that kept her there in the man's office. So she could be there for her aunt, when it mattered most.

Rae started back down the hospital corridor, only to become certain she wasn't ready to face the outside world. She veered right and followed the signs to the hospital cafeteria. She spotted her friend Olivia Reames seated with Cameron Tanner. The three of them had formed a close unit, meeting at least once each week, until Cameron's wedding the previous winter. Rae

decided sitting with friends and talking about anything except Emma would provide welcome support.
She went through the cafeteria line and selected items
she might keep down. This was going to be a very full
day, and lunch was part of her recovery. As long as
she didn't toss it all back up over her pals.

Olivia pulled out the neighboring chair and demanded, "Girl, who dropped a fly in your soup?"

"Doctor Asher. And to answer your next question,
no, I don't want to talk about it."

"I've heard the new doc possesses the kindly manner of a good suppository." Olivia grinned across the
table. "Isn't that right, Cameron?"

"It would be completely unprofessional to suggest
that particular colleague is a porcupine with a medical degree," she replied.

This was precisely the conversation she needed,
Rae thought. "How is your pregnancy going?"

"Oh, these final weeks are just a basket of warm
puppies." Cameron's smile was slightly canted. "And
if it doesn't end soon, my husband's hair is all going
to fall out."

"Well, now." Olivia's smile was far more genuine.
"Have you talked with Ursula in HR about your
hours after the little bundle pops out?"

"She happens to be my new best friend."

"Good girl." Olivia toyed with her spoon, her expression almost coquettish. "Okay, I give up. What did you and Brody talk about while I was on the phone?"

Rae straightened, looking from the pregnant clinician to the grinning pal. Started to ask exactly which Brody they were referring to, and whether it was the same one she was due to meet later that afternoon. A surprise addition to her crowded calendar. In the end, though, she wisely spooned her cottage cheese and fruit cocktail and stayed silent.

Cameron glanced at Rae and replied, "I'm not sure relating our conversation would be right and proper."

"Is he one of your patients?"

Cameron huffed. "Definitely not."

Olivia settled a hand on Rae's shoulder. "It may interest you to know that our dear Rae is another lady branded by my brother."

Cameron's gaze sharpened. "Is that so?"

Rae shook her head. "I'm sitting here because I'm interested in listening. Not talking."

"I suppose we can offer the lady a temporary pass," Olivia said.

"Okay, to answer your question, Brody asked me to help him find his way through personal changes."

Olivia's hand retreated to the table. "What kind of changes?"

"He didn't say."

"My brother. Asked you. About changing." A silence, then: "Did he mean it?"

"I'm certain he's sincere. Now, in this moment." A definite clinical element entered Cameron's voice. "But taking the hard long-term steps toward genuine bone-deep change?"

"You have your doubts."

Cameron nodded. "Is your mother going through with her divorce?"

Rae set down her spoon. She was so grateful for a reason to involve herself in other people's drama she could have hugged them both. Or wept. "I'm sorry, what?"

Olivia replied, "Mia moved out three weeks ago."

Cameron asked, "When did your brother learn about this?"

"Day before yesterday. Mom asked me to be there when she made the call. She wanted to be settled into her new apartment so she could invite Brody down for Christmas, just like she does every year. Keep this as calm and natural as possible."

"Can I ask why?"

"Because Brody likes to take charge of problems. He's done this all his life. Helping out, even when it's not wanted." Olivia had lost her smile. "Mom didn't want Brody becoming involved. It would wreck what-

ever shred of relationship he still has with his father."

Cameron was thoughtful now, every inch the professional. "What is his profession?"

Olivia shook her head. "The only profession Brody's
ever had is sailing. Everything else is gravy."

"His job, then."

"Something technical. He doesn't like to talk about
it. I think he's embarrassed over how little progress
he's made outside of ocean sailing—which is as close
to an addiction as my brother has ever come. I know
he works in Charlotte. I know he's got some kind of
technical job that grants him time to compete and
still pays him enough to have a place of his own."
Olivia shrugged. "That's it."

Cameron asked, "How often does he come back
for Christmas?"

"Every year he's not off racing."

"To answer your question, I think Brody has been
brought up short by your mother's actions. It has
shaken his world to the point where he is questioning
other aspects of his life. In time Brody will recover,
and he will resume the only course he's taken his entire adult life. His interest in the sort of change that I
represent will vanish. Smoke in the wind. Poof and
gone."

Olivia nodded slowly, keeping time with Cameron's words. "Will you help him?"

"Help is definitely the wrong word here. I will be there for him as long as he's interested in talking." She cast a glance in Rae's direction, then added, "Despite everything."

"Thank you." Olivia was somber now. "From the sounds of things, Brody needs you."

"And I'm there for him." Cameron glanced at her watch and rose from the table. "Who knows? Our conversations might even last through Christmas."

Brody left the hospital and continued east by north along highway 70, crossing the Radio Island bridge and then the newer structure linking Morehead to Beaufort. This time of year, the tourist traffic was manageable. He cruised down Front Street until he found what he sought, then swung inland and rounded a block, and parked by the Beaufort Grocery, an upscale restaurant occupying an eighteenth-century structure. He walked away from the water, went down two blocks, then came up where the live oaks cast shadows strong enough to keep him hidden.

There it was, moored off the town's main park and the Dock House restaurant. The new boat that was his for the taking. *Atlantic Winds* had been manufactured in the Netherlands by the world's preeminent builder of carbon-fiber hulls. The specially designed mast, constructed from the same superstrong material, rose to seventy-seven feet. So tall it could not pass under the majority of US bridges, where sixty feet was the maximum height allowed. Not that this restriction bothered Brody's boss.

Jacob Whitinger was determined to win the prize that had long eluded him. The Atlantic Cup was second only to the America's Cup, the world's oldest international sporting contest. The Atlantic Cup consisted of a race from Charleston to Newport, Rhode Island, followed by a second leg to Portland, Maine. Jacob had never won.

First prize carried a whopping sum of fifteen thousand dollars.

Brody had heard *Atlantic Winds* had cost just shy of two million dollars. And another two for outfitting and crew. Which Jacob was more than happy to pay— so long as they won.

The boat's size and length of shape and so much else was spelled out in the Atlantic Cup rulebook. But just as with Formula One, there remained a certain amount of latitude. Or wiggle room, as Brody's boss liked to call it.

Some people might say spending four million dollars for a winner's trophy and fifteen thousand dollar prize money defined overkill.

Those people did not know Jacob Whitinger. Or the fanatical determination required to win at ocean racing.

Sooner or later, Brody needed to check with the crew he had helped put together. They knew what he had told his company, that he needed time to deal with a family emergency, something so serious it kept him from completing the initial check of their new craft. All that was true and not true. From his shadowy hideaway, Brody listened to the crew's excited chatter, all of them happy with the down-east gift of unseasonably warm weather. Five days to Christmas, and the midday temps approached eighty degrees.

The boat's mooring said everything anyone needed to know about Jacob Whitinger. There was an excellent marina just beneath the new bridge. But no one outside the seaborne community ever went there. Most visitors had no idea how to find it. Which was why Jacob paid top dollar to moor where the entire world could come and stare and watch his wealth on display.

Brody wondered at his absence of any emotion. It was like staring at the boat of an old friend, someone he once knew. This craft and the prospect of racing simply did not hold him. He stood there, waiting to feel some draw, or regret. Anything that might suggest what next step he should take.

Instead, he felt nothing. There were no tidal currents pushing him in any particular direction. Regret, indecision, certainty over what he should do next, all that remained absent.

So far, his only concrete step had been that family-crisis email to his boss. Nothing more. He could easily step back into his role of number two on the new soon-to-be-winning boat.

And yet . . .

He returned to his car and drove back through Morehead City, then took the island bridge to Atlantic Beach. Brody parked in the lot bordering the town's small office district, then sat there, wondering at how a lifetime of yearning and struggle had brought him here: five days before Christmas, preparing to tear down everything he had spent years building up.

When it was time, Brody walked the two blocks to Rae Alden's offices. A youngish woman he vaguely recalled greeted him with the genuine warmth of an almost forgotten friend, and informed him that Rae was busy with a client call. The offices were bright and fresh, and a miniature Christmas tree sat front and center on an otherwise empty second desk. Brody was surprised and pleased to find the same print that adorned his home office on Rae's side wall. It suggested a connection that defied the silent years, one strong enough to spark a faint flavor of hope.

His earlier relationship with Rae Alden had been as close as Brody had ever come to true love. Despite all the reasons to the contrary, including years where their only contact was a quick hello between old friends, seeing this painting on Rae's wall brought up a surge of old emotions. Which was ridiculous, and Brody knew it. He tucked away those teenage absurdities just as Rae opened her office door.

3

Following the hospital visit, Rae returned to her office and accepted what had become a normal sheaf of message slips. Unless she was working on a tight deadline or crucial court filing, she rarely used her office cell. Carrying two phones was another part of this new existence, especially with Emma's health issues.

Rae could not be bothered to wait until safely inside her office to check the messages. Lana, her PA and friend, was the holder of multiple secrets, legal and otherwise. She said, "You know I would have texted your private number if Holden had called." Lana was also a happily married mother of three who thought Holden Geller was a perfect example of why good women went temporarily insane. "I take it you did give him your private number."

Rae let her hand drop. The messages weighed a ton. "Of course. But still."

Lana sniffed. "I could always loan you Scott's deer rifle. Give that louse the welcome he deserves when he finally shows up."

Rae let the comment go. "I need to make a couple of calls."

Lana checked her online calendar. "You have a Mister Brody Reames due in a few minutes."

"Have him wait."

"Should I start a file?"

"Probably not." Rae shut her office door and stood there, waiting in futile hope that her world would settle to a stable course, or answers appear in the sunlight streaming through her windows—something . . .

Following the treasure hunt that saved the Fortunate Harbor complex, Rae had been seeing Holden Geller whenever he was not away on some mystery assignment. "Treasure hunt" was how everyone involved now referred to the series of events that all crammed into a tight window of time and upended her life in the process. Saving Fortunate Harbor from the clutches of a truly bad man; uncovering a treasure of an even worse bad guy; Holden proving himself to be a mercenary with honor as well as good looks; Rae becoming the attorney of record for the Crystal Coast's first five-star resort; defying the DEA and coming out with her skin intact . . . "Treasure hunt" worked as well as anything.

Rae had any number of words to describe this new

version of her life. "Interesting" was what she mostly said when asked. Other terms came to mind, given the hour. Fulfilling. Frantic. Fun.

Lonely.

Most days, Rae remained too busy to worry about solitude. Her life was as full of people as she cared to make it. Days held conferences and planning sessions and court. Evenings, there were dinners and receptions and quite a few dates, especially with Holden.

But the nights were much too quiet, the hours overlong. Dawn runs had become her means of cutting short the empty space she couldn't fill.

Just the same, she had remained mostly happy, in a somewhat lonely and discontented manner. Those close to her assumed it all came down to two items: Rae's independent streak and breaking up with Jack, her beau until the previous spring. But Rae had made it this far being as honest as possible, especially with herself. And the truth was, losing Jack left her feeling nothing at all. Not even relief.

When she thought about Jack, which wasn't often, Rae found herself struggling to explain how she could have been with the man for ten months, fielded three marriage proposals, and liked him so much she had tried hard to call it love.

And yet, now . . . nada.

Her aunt Emma was the only person with whom Rae had shared the truth: It was like she'd been reading a good book, then finished a chapter, and turned the page. Did she miss the chapter now that it was over?

That was how she felt about Jack.

Holden and his entire team had once been Marines. Now they served as security for whoever could afford their fairly outrageous fees. In bygone eras, privateers had been buccaneers licensed by whichever nation controlled the waters near a particular island or stretch of mainland. The Crystal Coast had been claimed by Spain and Britain both, and this had once allowed pirates to wreak havoc in the offshore trading lanes. Some historians even claimed the worst of these brigands had secretly been granted semilegal status, at least for a time. In truth, Holden was nothing like that. He was one of the most honest and principled men Rae had ever met. But he still walked dark ways and wrapped himself in mystery.

Holden Geller was, in Rae's opinion, the penultimate good-bad boy. He and his crew had been essential in finding the treasure and rescuing the resort. He had then proven chivalry was in fact not dead, by allowing the rightful owners to keep it all. Holden's crew treated the well-deserved bonus payments as early Christmas. As if they didn't deserve being rewarded for their honesty.

Rae had been fairly comfortable with never asking questions she knew Holden wouldn't answer. These mysteries were the perfect reason to maintain iron-clad boundaries around their relationship. Rae assumed Holden felt the same.

Emma would be the first to say that when it came to matters of the heart, Rae was an expert at wrong ideas and worse moves.

Case in point: Three weeks earlier, she and Holden had been dining at the resort, an unseasonably warm night allowing them to be comfortable on the restaurant's terrace. Rae had been worrying over Emma's current ailments being more than just another spell, something Emma had experienced as long as Rae could remember.

Which was when Holden had proposed.

Well, not in so many words.

Instead, Holden broke into her thoughts with, "Earth to Rae."

"Sorry." She smiled and reached for his hand. "Emma."

He nodded. Holden was one of the few people who knew how worried she was. "Change the subject?"

"Please. I'd be so grateful, I'd make this meal my treat."

Only he did not return her smile. His hand was ice cold, his fingers limp. "I'm becoming emotionally involved with you. I think of you all the time."

Okay, so she had been semi-desperate for something to pull her away from the worries that framed so much of her days and nights. But this? She swallowed against a sudden queasy moment. "Holden . . ."

"Let me finish, Rae. Please." His features were craven in the candlelight. Like he had reverted to his deepest nature, a half-tamed buccaneer who only partly fit into this day and age. "I really, really want to see us together. As a couple. Permanently."

Which was when Rae lost all ability to draw air from the night.

"I need to know, Rae. Do we have a future together?"

She knew it was time for her to respond. But her thoughts were a tornadic swirl. Incoherent.

As if that particular nail needed to be hammered again, Holden added, "A lifetime kind of future."

For an endless moment the sputtering candle and voices drifting from neighboring tables were the only sounds.

Then it all coalesced. Her thoughts, the night, the necessary response. As if somewhere in her mind's lonely recesses Rae had actually been preparing for this very moment.

At least, that was how it seemed later. After it was over, and she had retreated to her condo. Alone.

Rae resisted the urge to pull her hand away. She maintained the fragile bond. Her voice sounded incredibly calm to her own ears as she replied, "Holden, I have a question of my own. One that needs answering before I could possibly think seriously about the words you just used. Permanence. Future. Together."

She heard herself clearly now, the way she was using her professional voice. Not so much impersonal as calmly insistent. And totally in control. Holden noticed it, too. He tried to pull away. But Rae held him fast.

"My question is this. Do you actually *want* a life's partner? Do you even know what that means? Could you truly be happy or content or comfortable in a relationship without secrets? Would you be willing to inform said partner of every job before you and your team commit?"

In the hours and nights to come, that was the point where she always gave an internal wince. Using that legal term, *said*. Wrong word, wrong move. It definitely added an unnecessarily frigid note.

Holden was quiet for a time, then asked, "Anything else?"

There was, actually. "One more essential point. Would you be willing to relocate your company to Atlantic Beach? Morehead City or Beaufort could probably work, but no further away. Because this is my home. Come what may."

Needless to say, the evening ended soon after. There were awkward silences and unfinished sentences and meaningless smiles and a polite farewell kiss to Rae's cheek.

When it was over, Rae wondered if this was her permanent fate. To build memories around standing alone, watching all her men drive away.

Since then, Holden had not called.

Rae felt a strange sense of disconnect, meeting Brody Reames after so long. She was far removed from the young woman who had enjoyed nine important and passionate months in his company. Though Rae had long ago left that chapter, book, epoch, it was definitely interesting. Brody Reames, requesting her time. As an attorney.

Eight years ago, Brody had been a wildly magnetic and incredibly handsome free spirit. Born three centuries earlier, he would have captained a fast blockade runner, or been a seaborne smuggler, or dead. Brody had never been much of a fighter. That of course made the pirating profession a nonstarter. Just the same, Brody was a magical artist at handling anything with sails. Open waters were and would always be his first love.

Rae had secretly wondered whether Brody was truly a competitor at heart, despite his fanatical desire to win whatever race he entered. Sometimes, when they had been alone and bonded at heart level, she had suspected racing merely framed his passion in modern terms, joined him with other like-minded fanatics, and offered a reason to soar on canvas wings.

Brody had arrived at the perfect moment, at least as far as young Rae had been concerned. She was gradually recovering from the crushing loss of Curtis, her first love, after he had left the Crystal Coast and their lives had taken different courses. Rae accepted that she and Curtis were not getting back together, their promises of lifelong love sundered by currents and forces beyond their control. And there, in the bleak months of growing acceptance and moving on, Brody Reames had entered her world.

Brody's hair was naturally copper-brown and with constant sun and salt went almost white blond. Brody had always been fit, muscular, and cautious about his habits. Though they earned none of the public accolades or money, ocean racers held to a professional athlete's fitness. He had the clear thousand-yard gaze of his ocean breed. His tan was a permanent fixture. Rae tried to imagine him as he might be now. So many of the guys she'd grown up with had aged incredibly fast. It was the risk of living in paradise. Diving into the bottle, the pipe, the pills, the lines. As a result, with far too many of the men her age, their expressions plowed deep furrows, the eyes went dull, the body became flaccid and slow.

When she opened her door, Rae found herself relieved that at least this one guy hadn't lost his edge. "Hello, Brody."

His smile was the same as well, revealed mostly in

his gaze and how dimples appeared even when his lips scarcely moved. "Hello, Rae. Thanks for seeing me."

Lana did not actually drool, but her gaze certainly suggested more than the fleeting interest of a happily married lady. "Are you sure I can't get you something?"

"I'm good, thanks."

Lana's smile carried a mischievous glint. "Mr. Reames was admiring your artwork."

He tapped the frame. "'Dance Me to the End of Love.' I have it on my living room wall."

"Get out of town."

"I've loved it from the first time I laid eyes on it." But his smile was gone now, his gaze sad. He started to say something more, but in the end just touched the frame a second time and turned away.

Rae found herself wanting to confess how she had recently become tempted to take it down, tear the print from the frame, and burn it. There was too strong a hint of all the dances she had not seen to the end, or had ended before she was ready, or stopped before the music really started. She merely said, "Come on in."

There was a new stillness to Brody, a trait she found even more distinct than the way he did not fully smile. The easygoing nature had certainly been erased. Whether it was a temporary result of the troubles that brought him here or something more permanent she could not say. Either way, the stillness marked a deeper element. She asked, "What can I do for you?"

Brody did not so much sit in the chair as crouch. "My mother is getting a divorce. Knowing my father, it's bound to get very messy, very fast."

That was as far as Rae let him go. "I'm sorry. I don't handle divorces. Not even for existing clients."

"My mother already has a divorce attorney. I know because I asked."

"Then why are you here?"

Brody repeated, "I know my father."

The man's utter stillness, combined with that ocean-horizon gaze, was eerie. "And?"

"He's going to do something unexpected. Vile. He will be after a triple dose of revenge. First, for Mom leaving him. Second, for the shock she's inflicted. Third, for the way she's shattered his oh-so-perfect public image." Brody might as well have been reading last week's weather report for all the emotions he showed. "There's only one way to stop this from becoming a disaster for everyone involved. And that's if a counterattack is already in place. A response of such overwhelming force, he realizes to move forward would result in a second dose of public shame." Brody nodded slowly. "He'll back down. Pretend it never happened. Go quiet, at least for now."

Rae found she needed a moment to process. She had never met Brody's father. In the nine months of their wildly passionate fling, she had heard numerous people, including Emma, speak about both his parents. Her aunt referred to Brody's dad as *the little dictator*. Olivia, Brody's sister, had been five years ahead of them in school. They had only become friends when Rae returned after her law studies. Olivia and her mother were two branches of the same blooming tree, quiet and opinionated and patient and strong. Olivia had never, not once, spoken about her father.

Rae rose, crossed to the connecting door, and asked Lana, "Who's up next?"

She already had Rae's calendar on her screen. "Blythe Dixon. Titles and such for their current new build."

"Call her and ask if I can pop by later."

Lana's smirk resurfaced. "Shall I start a file?"

"Not yet. Maybe. We'll see."

"Oh, goodie." She lifted the phone. "You kids play nice."

When she turned back, Rae felt her legal face settle in place. It was time to be all business. She took her time positioning a chair close to Brody. She wanted him to see clearly how barriers were about to come down, whether he liked it or not. She accepted that the threat Brody feared could very well be real. The question she needed answered had to do with motive.

Rae asked, "Why are you here?"

"I don't understand. My father—"

"I'm not asking about that. Your father has to wait. First, I need to know who my client is."

Brody was dressed in what Rae considered a big-city take on sailing garb. Navy cotton trousers with a sharp crease, half-zip matching sweater with a logo she didn't recognize, shiny black lace-up walking boots that could well have been designed by Coach. His hair was trimmed, his eyes clear. But the man's stillness took on a new element. Rae was pretty sure he actually winced.

When he remained silent, Rae pressed, "I met with your sister earlier. She was asked what you did, your job. She had no idea what to say. Why is that?"

Brody's lips parted, but no sound emerged.

"Do you understand why I'm asking? I can't involve myself in anything that even hints at illegality."

"It's nothing like that."

"Then why—?"

"I don't like talking about myself."

"If you want me to consider accepting you as a new client, you're going to have to do just that." Rae thought his expression could best be described as that of a deer in headlights, one second from impact. "Who are you, Brody?"

He rose, crossed the room, stared out the sunlit window. "Where did you see my sister?"

"We've been friends for years. We met today for a coffee at the hospital cafeteria."

"Then you know." Brody directed his words to the side window. "Olivia and Mom were the strong ones in our family. They stayed. They remained intact. I couldn't do that. Even before I was old enough to understand, I knew if I stayed around, I'd be lost."

Rae started to instruct him to return to the topic at hand, then decided to watch and see where this stranger was headed.

"Olivia protected me when I was little. Mom's done it all her life. It's my turn now."

"Your sister doesn't want you involved. Neither does your mother."

Brody glanced over. "I realize that. It's why I'd rather they not know I'm working with you. If I'm wrong, as far as they're concerned, our discussions never happened." He turned back to the window. "But all that is secondary to protecting them when Dad strikes. Which he will."

"Come sit down." When he remained stationary, standing with his face bathed by the winter light, she decided not to press. "Same question. What do you do professionally, and why—"

"I've spent my entire life hiding. I started wearing a mask at home. It defines me. Dad didn't even know I was racing until my team won the Bermuda challenge."

Now they were getting somewhere. "When was that?"

"I'd just turned seventeen. He read it in the paper. Local boy does good." His features might as well have been carved from the light. "I waited weeks for him to say something. He never did. Just started watching me differently."

She said it again. "Brody, please. Sit."

This time he obeyed. "You remember anything about me and math?"

Rae started to deny it, then: "I remember how you poured over wind and tide charts. You were always scribbling. I asked. You made a joke about it."

"It's always been my second love. I don't even remember when I started fooling around with math puzzles and online challenges."

Rae reached to her desk for a legal pad and pen, just to give her hands something to do. "So. Math."

"Applied mathematics. Working those charts was how I got accepted into the big winning boats at such an early age."

"And now?"

The furtive look, the stonelike expression, the fear, all returned. "Is this absolutely necessary?"

"Do you want me to represent you?"

"It's not a question of want. My mother and sister need—"

"This goes way beyond semantics," she countered. "If you want my assistance with a legal matter, I need to know what you do, and how you got there."

Which was both true and not true. But still.

Brody took a long breath. Released it slowly. Again. And he told her.

4

Twenty minutes later, Rae walked him back outside. Brody's revelations had left her wanting to conclude their time together with a signature move. Do something that showed him how impressed she was, and how touched.

The wind had switched to straight east and now carried a wintry bite. She thought Brody looked washed out and fragile from the confession. Which was remarkable, given what he had revealed. The man was still the boy, at least in some regards. Rae found herself respecting him for breaking the self-made mold in order to shield his sister and mother.

Standing on the empty sidewalk in front of her office, the island town might as well have been all theirs. Which was when she spotted the Land Rover with the dark-tinted windows.

It could have been anyone. Land Rovers were fairly common during the high season. A number of homeowners drove them. But this was five days to Christmas, and a slow-moving Rover on an empty island road inevitably brought Holden and his silence to mind.

She knew exactly what was required.

Rae said, "Have dinner with me tonight."

Brody's features flashed with very real pleasure. "I'd like that, Rae. A lot."

"Seven o'clock. Fortunate Harbor. My treat." As he thanked her and turned away, she added, "You need to speak with Olivia. And your mother. Tell them what you've told me."

"Rae, no—"

"Brody, they need to know who you are. What you do. You owe them that."

Another long breath, as if accepting her words was an act of pure defeat. Then, "Will you do it?"

She wanted to press. Demand that he take this on. Ask why it was so hard to give them what, in truth, was good news. Instead, his look of fearful desperation left her unable to say more than, "If you're absolutely certain that's what you want."

"I need this. Please, Rae. It would mean the world."

"I don't understand."

Rae and Olivia were meeting together for their regular Thursday evening drink. Usually this happened somewhere close to the hospital, so Olivia could pop in, share a laugh and a story about her day, then head home to husband and kids. This evening Cameron joined them, re-forming the trio that had framed so much of Rae's adult life. Olivia had two adorable daughters, both of whom were still in the munchkin age. The eldest, Rae's goddaughter, was about to turn six and showed distinct signs of becoming a Frozen-style princess.

Tonight, Rae had asked if they could shift to the Fortunate Harbor's main bar, since she was meeting Brody in an hour and a half. She had not yet mentioned this to either of her closest friends. She would probably tell them later. They already knew most chapters of her somewhat sordid romance saga, but not this particular page.

As part of the ongoing contract necessary to repay their work during the treasure hunt, Holden's crew remained on semipermanent retainer with the resort. Rae knew Holden would soon hear from whoever served on duty tonight. Rae couldn't say whether she preferred for Holden to view this news as pressure to redefine his idea of a real union or head for the exit. Which was probably a terrible thing to confess, even to herself. But as Rae lifted her glass, she was simply happy to have options. Not to mention how much she secretly looked forward to seeing Brody again.

Out of the office. Hopefully in a situation where she might peel away another couple of layers.

If Rae were ever to design her perfect bar, this place would definitely serve as a model. Tall windows overlooked a dusk-clad veranda rimmed by real torches in metal stands. She knew the wind had died, because the flames were not just stable but cheerfully inviting. Beyond the terrace rose coastal pines. A veil of sea oats were turned silver in the moonlight. The candle-lit bar was a perfect setting to share secrets and confess newfound love. If only.

She relished sitting here with two of her closest friends. Telling them about Brody's afternoon confession added a spice years in the making.

Olivia's features shifted in the candlelight as she took in Rae's words. "Tell me again what it was he specialized in?"

"Econometrics," Rae repeated. "I looked it up. It's the mathematical analysis of economic and market trends. Brody also completed a master's degree combining econometrics with international finance. According to him, they make a logical fit."

Olivia asked, "Why wouldn't he tell us?"

Cameron asked, "You're sure your mother doesn't know?"

"Mom wouldn't keep something like that from me," Olivia replied.

Cameron was seated on Olivia's other side. She leaned forward so as to focus on Rae. "I'm not clear on why Brody decided to treat you as his confessor."

"It wasn't like he volunteered. He came to me with a legal issue. I told him I'd help only if I had a handle on who he was." She looked at Olivia and said, "This afternoon, the way you couldn't describe his job, that troubled me."

Olivia lifted her glass. "Get in line."

Cameron nodded. "You were concerned he might be involving you in something illegal."

"Not Brody," Olivia said. Her features and voice both descended into sadness. "Not in a million years."

"I had to be certain." Rae hated how she had made her dear friend so unhappy. "It tore him apart, telling me. Years of barriers coming down."

Olivia asked, "You're sure his legal issue isn't about Mom's divorce?"

"I told you, I don't handle divorces." She hid her half-lie in another sip of wine. "He asked me to tell you something else. It has to do with why we met. Brody has been working for this same group in Charlotte since completing his graduate work. The owner is another sailing junkie, those were Brody's words. His boss skippers one of the top pro-am . . ."

Rae stopped talking when Olivia drained her glass,

gathered up her purse, and slipped from the stool. "I better be going."

It was Cameron who held their friend in place with a gentle hand on her arm and the simple word, "Wait."

Olivia did not reseat herself, nor did she meet anyone's gaze. But she remained there, listening.

Cameron asked, "The situation with your father, growing up, was hard on Brody?"

" 'Hard' doesn't begin to describe it. He never beat us or anything." Olivia's gaze was fixed on something far beyond the bar. "Brody was this sweet little kid. He was born on Christmas Eve, so Mom called him our Christmas sea-sprite. Our father terrified him."

Cameron's grip tightened. "I see this more often than you can imagine. Sensitive children shield themselves from an impossible situation by developing two different lives. The outside life, what they reveal to others, has little or nothing to do with their interior world. Too often what binds the two together is rage. Unbridled, unfocused, and very destructive. In Brody's case, it's his sport. Does that make sense?"

Olivia's only response was to slide back onto her perch. Staring at distant memories.

Cameron continued, "Then something happens. A change so monumental it fractures this double life. Your mother's divorce—" She stopped when Rae shook her head. "What?"

"It's more than that," Rae said. Stepping over the attorney–client line because Brody had asked her to. "Brody's boss has turned sailing into a cage. Your brother has finally decided he has no choice but to walk away from what he's considered his dream come true. His ideal world has become a nightmare. And he doesn't know what to do."

5

Brody arrived at Fortunate Harbor half an hour early. He walked around the main building, glanced inside, and spotted Rae seated at the bar with Cameron and his sister. He backed away until he was certain the lengthening shadows fully enclosed him. He walked the crossover and stepped to where the retreating tide left a strip of hard-packed sand. He had spent countless happy hours standing right here, in the space where it all came together. Ocean and shore and sky and wind and tomorrow.

Most sailors avoided the open waters. Either they sailed the inland waterway or they held to tidal currents and kept the shore in sight. Brody had never felt that way. He wasn't like some sailors he knew, who treated fear as a vice, an ailment they were immune to. Brody had been terrified more times than he could count. It was part of being out where human control of the situation could be erased in a split second. Where waves could go from rough to higher than the mast in a few minutes. He accepted the risk and the fear that came with it because it was the price necessary. His passion required an ability to look beyond fear and do whatever it took to survive. Because the alternative was simply out of the question. Stand on the shoreline, remain landlocked and stationary while the open waters and the wind sang their siren's melody.

To an outsider viewing the carefully constructed script of Brody's existence, the single glaring flaw these days was his social life.

He didn't have one.

His time in competition meant he was simply unavailable for what normally passed as a working relationship. Unless, of course, his partner was either some angelic being who was able to cope with his absences and the risks they carried, or a crew member on the same boat. And the prospect of yet more casual temps, as he had secretly come to call them, left Brody feeling ancient at thirty. This semi-enforced solitude was one of the few steps he'd recently taken that carried a genuine rightness. Or harmony. Something.

The gathering night became stained by faces he scarcely recalled. These same images had forged the reasons why he stood here tonight, alone and seeking a way out. Knowing it was time to flee the life he had struggled to make his reality.

He checked his watch and saw it was time to meet Rae. He took the wooden path back across the barrier dunes and spotted her seated alone at the bar. The sight brought him to a standstill. A single candle illuminated her features. She sat with shoulders hunched and face creased by emotions she probably assumed no one could see. The bar's shadows looked ready to swallow her whole.

Another man was watching Rae. Brody had spotted him standing beneath a different boundary palm while leaving the parking lot. The man had shifted closer to the bar now, holding to the peripheral shadows. Brody had seen a lot of professional bodyguards; the ocean racing scene was a gathering spot for the superrich. But this guy was different in how he watched Rae.

Then Brody spotted his boss.

The restaurant terrace was gradually filling up. Tall heating lamps were now stationed among the tables and a chest-high Plexiglas wall held back the ocean chill. At a table on the terrace's far end, the CEO of Brody's company was holding forth, probably entertaining a group of sponsors and their wives. The man's capped teeth shone in the light as he completed his story and was rewarded with loud laughter. If he noticed Brody crossing the terrace and entering the bar, he gave no sign.

Which was just like the man. Continuing the pattern Jacob Whitinger had maintained since Brody joined the company and his racing team. Doing what came naturally, keeping his staff in their place.

Making sure Brody understood the boundaries of his life.

Rae had spotted Brody when he climbed the beach crosswalk and entered the hotel's exterior lights. If he noticed one of Holden's team standing further along, Brody gave no sign.

She regretted everything about the night now. Agreeing to be Brody's spokesperson had saddened one of her closest friends. Not that Rae was any better in the honorable-action department. She sighed into her empty glass. Wishing the night was already over.

Brody approached, but remained standing. "What's wrong?"

"I shouldn't ever have agreed to speak on your behalf." She pushed her glass toward the hovering bartender. "You made me hurt my oldest and dearest friend."

Brody sighed his way down onto the neighboring stool. "I should have seen that coming."

"Yes, Brody. You should have."

"I'm trying to correct some of my lifetime mistakes." When the bartender set down her freshened glass, he pointed and raised his finger. "I'm really, really sorry. It only made things worse."

"You can't avoid being honest, if honesty is what you're after." Rae caught a glance of herself in the bar's rear mirror. She huffed a bitter laugh. Listen to her, giving advice to this guy. What a joke.

"No, you're right." They sat together, mired in a glum silence that both joined and separated. Finally, Brody offered, "We can call tonight off if you want."

"What I want is to know the truth." She ignored how Holden's guy had shifted over to where he now stood in the exterior lights, clearly wanting to catch her eye. "What on earth happened to you?"

Brody thanked the bartender, sipped his wine, said, "One of the first lessons the Outer Banks taught me was, sometimes life can be too perfect."

Rae lifted her glass, drank, said, "That sounds more familiar than you will ever know."

"The summer before I turned fourteen, my uncle Travis gave me a summer job as dock boy."

Rae recalled a burly man with a seaman's smile so constant, the creases fanning from his eyes and mouth shone bone white when he frowned. "I remember him."

"He ran the Island Marina and Boatyard. For fifteen dollars a week I worked dawn to whenever. My job was to do whatever anybody told me. I was in heaven. Travis threw in all the sailing time I could manage in the idle hours. When he saw I worked first and sailed second, he started teaching me how to race. Centerboard hulls, that was his passion. I spent that first season crewing on his Dutchman. Two years later, I was racing the marina's Finn."

"And winning." Rae recalled watching Brody race, the sheer unbridled joy he brought to the sport. "You were great."

Rae thought the compliment made him sadder still. "Four years later, I was head dockhand and sailing instructor. And I was crewing on the top local ocean racer. With my tips and salary, I was pulling in around four hundred bucks a week. I was driving Travis's old Jeep and living in a studio apartment above the shop."

Rae nodded, a tiny gesture. She remembered that apartment.

"I was ready to put a downpayment on a new Mustang convertible, the Shelby Cobra model. Three sailing buddies and I were looking for a place on the island to rent." He hesitated, glanced at the windows leading to the restaurant terrace, then forced out, "I surfed, I sailed, I fished, I had a second boat offering me their top slot. It was the only life I knew, the only one I ever wanted."

The man, the life, this was what she remembered about Brody. She even remembered the friends, how they made their search for a place part of the never-ending joyride. Only now this man she once knew had to force out the words, an evening confession that had him sweating. And something more. Every time he glanced out the bar's rear windows, he tensed.

Not that looking outside was any reason to party for Rae. Tonight's guard on beachside duty was Ellis, one of Holden's senior crewmembers. Ellis remained where the spot lit him like a human statue. Watching. Which of course was what she had hoped would happen. Back when she thought it was the right move, meeting Brody here.

She asked, "What's out there on the terrace that worries you?"

He was as grim as she'd ever seen. "My boss."

"The one you say is trying to keep you in a cage." When he nodded, she went on, "I have to tell you, that doesn't make a lot of sense. Why don't you just quit?"

He kept nodding. "I probably should have taken that step long before now."

"So?"

Brody's only response was to hunch over his drink. The position reminded Rae of a child fearing a blow. For the first time that night, Rae was fully connected to the place and time. "Brody, look at me." When he glanced over, she told him, "You're not in this alone.

I know it's hard to open up. But you need to. Really. Trust me to help you find—"

"I started working for this group straight out of grad school. Jacob Whitinger is well known in sailing circles. He's a top-flight competitor, his boats are the latest in design, his crew as good as they come. To be invited to join them was a dream come true." He lifted his glass, then set it down. "I've known for years he wasn't paying me what I deserved. But the racing made that almost okay. Until three months ago."

"What happened?"

"I was invited to give the keynote address at a major conference. Totally out of the blue. Being included as a speaker is like having an international spotlight put on my professional standing. And not just me. The firm is treated as a headliner." His words were one thing. His position totally another: his gaze was flat now, his forehead beaded with sweat. "Jacob was furious."

She could feel his tension in her own gut. It required real effort to keep her voice steady. "What can you tell me about him?"

"In the private investment universe, Jacob Whitinger is a major player." The hand that lifted his glass sent tremors through the liquid. "When I returned from the conference, Jacob screamed at me. I couldn't understand it. I had sent the standard sort of memo, saying I'd been invited and was heading out. I went to conferences like this four or five times each year. No biggie. The only reason I mentioned it to Jacob was, you know, kudos and all that. The day I got back, he was so furious he could hardly get the words out."

Rae thought she could give the man's attitude a name. "You'd discovered a way out of his cage."

"I didn't know it then. But two weeks later, yeah, one of our major competitors offered me a job. Almost double my salary."

She could read the answer now. "If you accept, you lose your position on Jacob's boat."

"It's a lot worse than that." Brody drained his glass. "I can race because Jacob doesn't count the time against me. If you factor in training and trials, that makes up almost three months every year."

The man's tension could no longer touch her. She was incredibly grateful for this moment, the opportunity to move beyond her own splintered motives and focus on her client's genuine need. "He's holding that over you, isn't he." When he did not respond, she demanded, "What has he done, Brody?"

"Refused my end-of-year bonus. Almost a third of my salary." Brody lifted his glass, realized it was empty. Held it toward the bartender. "Told me I wasn't performing up to standard."

Rae rose from her stool, waved away the bartender. "Let's go."

Brody jerked as if coming awake. "Rae, I'm sorry, I shouldn't have bothered—"

"Stop. Just stop. We're going outside, we're having dinner, and we're talking next steps." When he remained seated, uncertain, worried, she tugged on his arm. "Come on, sport. It's time to mess with that man's night."

6

The evening was so still the external heaters formed a welcoming cloud of warmth. The terrace held a rough-hewn, almost pagan feel. Illumination from table candles and torches rimming the terrace caused the diners to dance and weave while seated. Each table was an island, as intimate a setting as ever designed by man.

Brody floated behind the waiter, guided by Rae's hand on his arm. He was caught unawares by the onslaught of emotions he thought dead and buried. He had no idea why he had spoken like he did. The words had felt drawn from some hidden depths, opened by the presence of this woman. Rae was no longer the college girl he had fallen in love with. She was that and more besides. Holding onto secrets did not fit with the night. Brody knew full well this was probably a singular event. For her, it was a chance to renew an old acquaintance, come to know her new client a little better. He was so unaccustomed to feeling anything at all in a woman's company, the experience left him defenseless. She asked, he answered. It was that simple.

Rae directed him into a seat so that his back was to the table where his boss held forth. Just the same, he could feel the man's ire, strong as the terrace's heat keeping the ocean chill at bay. He asked Rae to order for them and pretended to listen as she and the waiter discussed the night's specials. He accepted the wine list, asked for a suggestion, agreed, all without really making conscious note of what was said. Now that they were seated and she faced him across the expanses of linen and glittering silverware, her presence enveloped him.

The years had refined and strengthened Rae Alden, and the result was a far lovelier woman. Stable, centered, utterly aware. Rae's eyes were a remarkable wash of deepest green, her hair a cultivated blend of brown and auburn. She wore it long and draped over her left shoulder. She had come straight from work, and her navy suit was somewhat creased from a stressful day. The long hours only accentuated her determined strength. He breathed, and caught a hint of her scent, an enticing mélange of what would never be his.

Rae said, "I want you to forget about the man over there. If Jacob decides to insert himself into our night, it's his choice. Unless that happens, he does not exist. He does not enter into the equation. Okay?"

Because it was Rae who asked, he replied, "I'll try."

When she paused, Brody knew she was about to pose another highly personal question. What amazed him the most was how little he minded.

His world of high-wire tension and fast money contained a multitude of liars. The 24/7 realm of global markets was home to people who eagerly redefined themselves. They built an external myth, a shell that declared to outsiders that here was a ruler of the moneyed universe. In contrast, Brody didn't lie. He simply hid in plain sight. He let people think what they wanted. Yet he held one trait in common with so many of his fellow traders: Brody had no idea who he was at life's deepest levels.

Whatever it was she wanted to know, he would tell her. The answer was there in his heart and mind, seemingly before she even posed the question. As if he had waited years for this night, this hour, this woman.

Just the same, there was one thing he had to know. "Did you ever marry?"

She reversed course. Brody saw it in her eyes, like reading an incoming shift in the wind by watching the tiny wavelets, the feathering effect of change. He half-expected her to say it was none of his business. Which was fair enough. This was not some arrangement where she had to give in response for getting.

But when she spoke, it was to ask, "You remember when we met, I was still recovering from an early flame."

He did, in fact, which revealed how Rae had branded his heart. Brody had known from the outset that some guy had hurt her badly. Shattered that gemstone gaze and left her determined to avoid future entanglement. Rae had never said a word, of course. And Brody had done his best to offer the good-time comfort she was after. "Curtis—do I remember that right?"

Her eyes glinted with momentary humor. An ideal moment to comment over how he remembered such details after so long. Instead, she said, "I never told you what it meant to become involved with you. How you helped me heal. Look beyond what hadn't worked out."

Actually, she had. But Brody did not want to risk breaking the momentary spell of shared intimacy. Even when it hurt to have their time together packaged around the shadow of her previous love. He remained silent.

And he remembered.

Brody had offered Rae what he hadn't to so many others. He tried to think of her first, a new concept as far as he was concerned. With Rae, though, it had felt natural. Because he had fallen in love.

Rae continued, "I had a couple of close calls, once

in law school and another here. My lawyer flame had his heart set on the big city. And I'm an island girl. Come what may." She smiled at the waiter setting down their first courses, and when they were alone again, she went on, "Then there was Jack."

He hated the guy already. "Uh-oh."

Between bites, Rae described the relationship that had been over for almost nine months and seemed like much longer. Brody ate mechanically. The excellent food was secondary to what she was saying. He mostly feasted on this rare chance to share an intimate moment. Despite how his ardor was not reflected back in her voice or gaze. And never would be.

"This probably sounds terrible and callous and cold," she told him. "There were a dozen reasons why we could have made a go of it. But the truth was, our relationship never truly captured my heart or my mind. When he broke it off, I admit it hurt. But not for long. And not all that much."

Brody felt encased in the wonder of a night he never thought would happen, not in a million years. Seated here with Rae, relishing how she shared her heart. In this moment, the candles and the starlight and the blanketing warmth and the ocean's siren whisper. It was enough.

She looked up, offered a fractured smile. "Sorry."

"For what? Rae, I really appreciate—" He stopped

because she straightened in her chair and looked beyond him.

Instantly, Brody knew his boss was on approach.

Rae set her napkin on the table. "Do you have representation for this upcoming negotiation?"

Brody felt himself drawing away. Their intimate evening was over, replaced by the same indecision and worry he had lived with for over a month.

Rae shocked him by reaching across the table. She gripped his hand and said softly, "Pay attention and answer my question."

"Rae, there's no negotiation. I don't even know what representation means." There was a great deal more he could say. How ultimatums formed Jacob's hardball negotiation tactics. Win at all costs. That was Jacob Whitinger.

But Rae had heard enough. She tightened her hold on his hand and commanded, "Stay seated. Don't speak. Trust me." She released him, pushed back her chair, rose to her feet, and took a step forward. Directly into Jacob Whitinger's path.

Sometimes it bothered Rae, how much she relished confrontations like this. She did not actually enjoy doing verbal battle. The question of pleasure did not enter in. This was something else entirely.

Growing up, she had heard Curtis's dad and her

uncle talk about the difference between a cop and a civilian. How it was second nature to them, running toward trouble when everybody else fled. Putting their lives on the line for strangers. That was how Rae felt about the sort of conflict the legal profession required her to handle. In such situations, she came into her own. It was that simple.

The torchlight illuminated a man she instantly recognized. Jacob Witinger was a star in the financial world, one of the few who made North Carolina home. He was a frequent guest on televised business reports. Rae had heard him speak at the regional TED talk. He was often quoted in the *Journal*. He had adorned covers, his cleft chin and rugged features and handsome smile making for good press.

None of this mattered.

Jacob stepped in close, using his height and prowess to crowd Rae. Yet he ignored her entirely and instead focused on the younger man who had not yet looked his way. Clearly, he sought to intimidate Rae. Make her small and insignificant.

Good luck with that.

Jacob demanded, "Brody, who is this woman standing in my way?"

"Rae Alden," she replied. Courtroom voice, calm demeanor, utterly unfazed by the man's demeanor. "Attorney of record."

His expression suggested he'd just found something on the sole of his shoe. "Brody, what is this?"

"My client and I were discussing issues related to Mr. Reames's next steps."

His smile was as false as it was unwavering. "Brody, tell this woman her presence is unnecessary."

Rae pretended he had not spoken. "We would be happy to meet with you in the coming days, Mr. Whitinger. As soon as my client decides whether his professional life requires a move."

The chairman and chief executive officer of the southeast's largest investment fund was a global negotiator, a man rarely shaken by opponents seeking to blindside him. He offered Rae the sort of meaningless smile he might show a misbehaving child. Before the first strike. "In that case, I suppose it would cause me some minor regret to accept one of the multiple requests I'm fielding from prospective crew members."

Sometimes after a particularly intense courtroom battle, Rae woke in the early dawn and lay there remembering. She did not focus on the argument or what was said or the reasons for conflict. Instead, her mind became captured by the way certain elements had stood out. How she had been so intensely fastened inside the moment, she could have counted the beat of a hummingbird's wings. Every tiny aspect of the place, the opposing counsel, the judge, the jury, it was all embedded in her awareness. Just like now.

She heard the sputtering torches, the indistinct drift of conversation from other tables, the ocean's soft whisper. How the flickering light turned Whitinger's smile into a clown's mask. How his eyes held the color of flint. How his expression declared he was totally in control.

Wrong.

She replied, "Then we should probably thank you for making our analysis of options so much easier."

He hated having to ask. Just hated it. "Options?"

"Why we are meeting here tonight," Rae said. "Other groups have come forward, willing to pay Mr. Reames what he deserves."

"Do they also offer your client the *option* of continuing with his second career? I think not."

"Which is precisely why it would be in your best interests to reconsider your approach to my client," Rae countered. "Since he holds such importance to *your* personal goals."

"No crew member on *my* vessel is irreplaceable, Ms. . . ."

"That depends on how vital you consider the goal of winning, doesn't it, Mr. . . ."

That definitely worked under his skin. "The only crew member vital to winning races is the skipper. Myself."

"Is that your formal response?" Rae gave it a beat. "Instead of opening negotiations so that we can settle on what would prove to be a fairer offer. Which would naturally include two *nonnegotiable* elements."

The torches sputtered in tune to the rage Whitinger did his best to suppress. "I'm waiting."

"Payment of this year's bonus, which we both know he fully deserves." Rae might as well have been reading off a script she'd spent weeks preparing. "And written acknowledgment of my client's freedom to appear on whatever program, and speak at whatever event, that he feels—"

"That is not happening."

Rae responded with her best theatrical regret. Not fully suppressing her smile. A woman representing a client in high demand. And letting this blowhard know, in no uncertain terms, he was no longer in control. She plucked a card from her pocket and offered it with "I do hope you will reconsider that position. In which case, I look forward to discussing terms that guarantee this *irreplaceable* employee remains in a position where he both serves the corporate good and is available to crew whenever his services are required."

Whitinger despised needing to take her card. He glared a final time at Brody and replied, "We'll see."

He did not lose his smile as he backed away.

Once he melded with the shadows, Rae resumed

her seat. It would have been wrong to show any hint of delight over how the confrontation had played in their favor. Because she knew without looking that Whitinger was watching.

Brody, however, looked one step away from total meltdown. "What do you think you're doing?"

"Serving your best interests." She resisted the urge to renew her grip on his hand. "Smile at me. Pretend you've just won. Which, by the way, you just did."

"Rae, you don't know him. That man—"

"Is watching. Do what I say. That's it. You're having the time of your life." She reveled in the focused intensity, the power she had to make even Brody rise to the occasion. "When would your boss expect to hear from you next?"

A long moment, the torches hissing and breathing for him, then: "Tomorrow we should be starting ocean trials on our new vessel."

"You mean, *his* boat." She lifted her chin. "Take a drink from your glass." When he had done so, she continued, "Sometime before Christmas, we're going to go shopping for *your* new boat. Because, believe you me: when you don't show up for training, your boss will have someone track you. Hearing that you've begun scoping out what's available and on sale will tell him what we want him to know."

Brody's gaze carried a genuine confusion, as if he'd seated himself across from one woman and now found himself in the company of someone else entirely. "Which is?"

"The clock is ticking on Jacob Whitinger." Another uplift of her chin. "Finish your starter."

"I'm not hungry."

"Did I ask you that? No, I did not." Rae smiled as he picked up his fork. She sounded so much like Emma it was ridiculous.

Before she was able to give in to worry over her aunt's state, Ellis stepped closer to the veranda. Holden's crewmember stood silhouetted by the rising moon. Rae looked away and allowed herself a moment to ponder what it was she really wanted to see happen.

7

Brody had booked a room at the oceanfront Double-tree. The hotel was located at the opposite end of Atlantic Beach from Fortunate Harbor and his boss. Normally Brody stayed in whatever guesthouse they took for the crew. It was always nice enough, not luxurious but so large everyone had their own room. The socializing elements between ocean trials was crucial to a well-functioning team. But given the uncertainty over his future, the next-to-last thing Brody wanted was to show up there. And the very last was to go home. Spend the holidays with his dad. Not in a million years.

When he rose at daybreak, his sister had already texted. There was none of Olivia's normal warmth or welcoming cheer. My place. Nine o'clock. We're going to Mom's. You're driving. And you're talking. O.

Brody used the room's coffee maker and drank it black, eating a power bar for breakfast. It reminded him of so many great mornings, preparing for another day on the open water, charts spread out of the dining table, joking with his team as they drank bad coffee.

He drove up the central highway, his thoughts bouncing back and forth between the coming confrontation with Olivia and the previous night. Rae had astonished him. Brody had always avoided confrontation and conflict. It was a habit so ingrained it might as well have been part of his genetic structure. He recalled sitting at the table and watching Rae handle his boss. Looking back, it felt like he had been in the presence of a karate master, deflecting blows, redirecting the force, winning. When she resumed her seat, Rae had looked calmly satisfied. Like it was nothing. Like she feasted on power players every day of her working week.

Olivia was standing outside her Morehead City home when he pulled up. Her arms were wrapped around her middle, her face set. Like she was waiting to give one of her kids a very hard time. She had always been there for him. He had disappointed her. Brody rose from the car, walked around, held her door, wished her a good morning. He deserved what was coming next. No question.

But once they were underway, all she said was, "I'm waiting."

Soon as he read her text, he knew revealing secrets

would define his day. He could not redo the past. But he could try and do a better job with this moment. And apologize. If she decided to give him that chance. "You remember Uncle Travis."

"Mom's brother. Of course I do." Not so much angry as sullen. Sad. "You two were very close."

"He was a great boss, as long as you met his expectations. Travis was the kindest man . . ." His throat clenched shut. The memories of Travis teaching him how to sail were suddenly as vivid as the road ahead. His smile, the way he watched Brody, knowing and understanding. No need for either man to speak a single word. There for him. Brody's first true friend.

The marina had possessed a seedy lived-in atmosphere and smelled of wet canvas and fuel and fishing gear and salt. A world removed from the rigid confines of Brody's home. After he turned fourteen, Travis somehow arranged it so Brody could spend weekends in the ratty upstairs apartment. Those nights of quiet solitude, falling asleep to the whisper of ocean winds and lines rattling against masts, were his first taste of heaven. For years after he bade the Outer Banks a bitter farewell, his finest and hardest dreams always began with that nighttime melody.

Brody gradually refocused on the here and now when Olivia shifted position so as to watch him. She leaned against the side door, observing him with unblinking intensity. He offered, "Sorry."

Olivia did not respond.

"It was the summer before I left for college," he began. "Travis called me in after work. I thought, you know, I had done something wrong, he was so serious. He locked the door with us inside. Settled in his pilot's chair and just launched straight in. How he'd been married twice and jailed four times. Booze wrecked his life and ended his career in the navy. He washed up here a broken man."

Olivia said softly, "I don't understand."

"Neither did I. Travis said that he wasn't one for telling me how to live my life. But he had a question he wanted to pose. One he thought I should consider. I told him, sure. I wasn't certain I wanted to hear, but something about the way he revealed himself—"

"You trusted him."

Brody nodded. "He told me soon after he started working at the marina, his father died. A hard and bitter man, was how Travis described him. A lot of dark shadows that formed barriers between him and the world. A lot of reasons for how his only son took any chance he could to self-destruct."

Olivia said, "He could be talking about Dad."

"Exactly what I thought," Brody recalled.

"Why was he telling you this?"

"He never said. He was a lot like our mom, his sister, using silence as a part of any conversation."

"I remember that, too," Olivia said.

"I think he wanted me to know up front, if I chose to ignore what he was going to say, he wouldn't hold it against me. Not then, not ever."

Olivia asked, "What did he tell you?"

"Travis said I'd done a good job of building my idea of a perfect existence. He'd been watching me, and he was fairly certain I was strong enough to make a good island life for myself." Brody glanced over. "He said he was proud of me. I'd never had a man say that to me before."

Olivia remained still. Silent. Involved.

"But he reminded me that time does not stand still. Seasons change. I might've thought that summer season and the high life it brought me was permanent, but the experiences I loved might not always hold me like they did then."

Travis was there in the car with them. Riding east on 70, part of everything. Not just the memory. The here and now. It hit Brody hard as a blow to the heart, how so much of what he faced was a repeat of those earlier moments. Like today's crisis was what Travis had been talking about all along.

Brody glanced over, grateful for Olivia's patience. "He asked if this was enough. Not just for the one season, but for life. I needed to answer the question, before the season changed and the choice was made for me."

Olivia breathed. But did not speak.

"He said there was still time to do more, grow beyond where I was, change into a different person. And what I needed to figure out was, beyond the passion and the pleasure, whether my father was the one holding me in place."

Olivia was with him now. "Did you want more out of life?"

"Was I trapped in my good times like Travis had become caught up in the bad. Could I do what was necessary to break free, and did I want to."

"It makes sense now, his confession," Olivia said. When Brody did not respond, she added, "Mom needs to hear all this. Today."

Brody nodded, filled with an overwhelming desire to wind back the clock, to have this conversation years ago. Glad it was happening now.

Aching over all the lost time.

Olivia's incessant demand for answers was eventually satisfied. The longer they spoke, the more she accepted that he would reveal the hidden components of his life's story at his own pace.

But her sadness remained.

She glanced at her watch and said she needed to be back in time for her older daughter's recital that evening. Brody said he was glad to hear the little girl was holding to her passion for dance. Olivia asked where he was staying. He told her about the hotel room and a desire to distance himself from the crew. But he did not explain why, and she did not press. That part of the story would wait until their mother could hear it as well.

Olivia did not ask if he had seen their father.

The drive from Atlantic Beach to Oriental was a journey from shoulder to wrist, traveling around a crooked elbow. By air the distance was less than thirty miles. But the journey by car took well over an hour, first heading inland on 70 all the way to New Bern, then back east again on the smaller county highway 55. The distance in terms of place and epoch was even further. One small town after another came and went, shuttling the traveler through decades of quiet stability. Brody and Olivia gave in to the simple pleasure of belonging. Their silence was part and parcel of life in these down-east hamlets. The homes and shops fronting the highway were little more than anchors to what lay hidden down lanes branching out north and south, back to where dark waters rested in forested creeks that had remained unchanged for centuries. Atlantic Beach and the surrounding ocean-front growth, New Bern and its vibrant energy, all that was lost now. The ancient ribbed road framed by Spanish moss, the quiet orderly yards and the flags hanging from so many porches, all spoke of a different realm.

This was his mother's world. Her family hailed from Swansboro, a waterfront town set between Morehead and Jacksonville. Her parents were true downeasters, molded by generations beyond count. The original settlers hailed from northern Germany. Three centuries earlier they had traded frigid North Sea waters for the Outer Banks' inland reaches. They fished, they farmed, they held to traditions the outside world thought lost and gone forever.

Brody's grandparents had defined silence. His grandfather had been a skilled carpenter, which was how his parents had met. At the time, Brody's father had been supervising an expansion of military housing, and his grandfather had been responsible for the kitchens. Brody's grandparents could go an entire weekend without speaking a word. Their home was the only place where the younger Brody could spend hours in his father's company and feel safe.

Yachting magazine had recently named Oriental the nation's number-one small town for sailors, a secret most locals wished had never become public knowledge. There were signs of growth everywhere. Even so, the town itself remained steadfast in its connection to quieter, simpler times.

Mia Reames met them, as always, with hugs and soft words. Only the location had changed. Her home was a newly built condo at the point where Whittaker Creek met the Neuse River. The scent of brackish waters and rattle of halyards on sailing masts greeted them through her open balcony doors.

The condo was spacious and welcoming, the living room's hardwood floors decked out with woven rugs Brody did not recognize. The furniture was mostly new and old-fashioned at the same time. Mia Reames might as well have resided there for years.

Brody did not wait for his sister to push him into speaking. He seated himself in a new leather settee and began with a recital of what he had told Olivia. As he spoke, even more memories rose to the surface. When his uncle had fashioned the marina's upstairs studio into a haven for Brody, Travis had said nothing except that the young kid was welcome. His mother's brother would not permit Brody to criticize his parents' home, but he said nothing as Brody inserted himself ever further into the marina life.

The sun emerged from behind a passing cloud as Brody talked. Light struck the wind-dappled waters and reflected into Mia's new home. Colors played in a liquid flow across her ceiling, illuminating her simple chandelier. A Christmas tree between the fireplace and the balcony blinked in solemn cadence with Brody's telling. Mia and Olivia sat in two padded rockers he didn't recognize. As far as Brody could see, the only items his mother had brought from their for-

mer home were the sea-glass trinkets he had gathered
and fashioned as a child. Only now they were set
against matching pastel backings and framed in what
appeared to be hand-polished driftwood. They hung
on every parlor wall, surrounded by early pho-
tographs of him and his sister. The formal family por-
traits his father had annually insisted on were absent.

Mia punctuated the end of his first episode by offering her children lunch. Brody followed them into
the kitchen, feeling as if he saw the two women with
new eyes. As if his confessions had erased a veil he
had not even realized was in place. His mother wore
a patterned skirt and loose-fitting cotton sweater that
buttoned up the front. She was neat and precise in her
movements, an intelligent woman who was comfortable with people discounting her abilities, which were
many. For as long as Brody could remember, Mia
Reames had been the public face of her husband's
subcontracting business. She bid on projects for the
military bases, she shaped the work sheets, she ordered, she kept the office running smoothly. Where
possible, she poured her own personal unguent over
wounds her husband opened.

She served one of Brody's favorite meals, split pea
soup simmered and thickened for hours, flavored
with homemade chicken stock and butter-basted sor-
rel. Dessert was a bundt cake, using the cast-iron pan

her family had handed down for generations. A bundt pan was shaped like a giant donut, which meant extra crust in every serving. Mia flavored her cakes with double cream, crushed almonds, and baker's chocolate that oozed over Brody's fork.

They remained at the kitchen table as Brody delved further into long-held secrets. How his childhood fascination with numbers had not faded as his father and most others assumed. Travis had noticed the young boy's ability to add numbers faster than Travis could enter them into his calculator. He had challenged Brody to study inland tidal flows and weather forecasting and ocean currents. All were vital elements for anyone wishing to skipper an ocean racer, he explained, then watched as Brody had gobbled up everything his uncle could find.

Travis had then urged him to take online classes and enroll at the community college. As Brody described the delight of being challenged to delve further and grow faster, he saw how Olivia lost every last vestige of tension. His sister seemed to shrink, actually grow smaller as he talked. For Brody, it felt as though he dipped his toe into a fast-moving river. Testing the water, seeing for himself what existed beyond his long-standing boundaries.

When he paused for breath, Mia took the opportunity to rise and brew coffee. She spoke for the first time since inviting them into the kitchen. "Then Brother died."

"Twenty months after he challenged me," Brody confirmed. "Midway through my fifth term at Carteret Community."

Olivia asked, "How old were you?"

"A few weeks shy of my twentieth birthday," Brody replied, remembering. "And already head over heels in love with econometrics."

"I'm still having trouble understanding what that word means," Olivia said.

The simplest definition was a mathematical description of how people spent money. But what Brody discovered in those heady days was an entirely new world. The study of markets and stocks and bonds and commodities and currencies gave both structure and form to his love of math. He was moving beyond math for math's sake. The seas of international finance and markets were now his to navigate. He could build charts to define the coming storms and risks. He could define a lifetime of new quests.

Brody stopped, gave it a beat, then repeated his mother's words. "Then Uncle Travis died."

The event had rocked his world as few things ever had. And the timing could not have been worse.

The marina had long been owned by the international group currently seeking to acquire Beaufort's town docks. One of their regional managers stopped by every few months, checking the books, surveying the structures, giving employees the stink eye. Or so Brody thought, until the manager called and offered him the top job. At nineteen. Great salary, hours, and time off twice yearly for his racing fix. It was, in effect, a dream come true.

As a result, Brody descended into what felt like a self-made purgatory. The days and weeks that followed should have held a state of semipermanent bliss. Instead, Brody felt a restlessness that bit deep, working in his muscles and his attitude until he became trapped beneath his very own personal storm cloud.

And then the reason became clear.

Earlier that year, Brody had reluctantly allowed his econometrics prof to share his honors thesis with a friend on the Wharton faculty. A month and a half before Travis's passing, he had been invited up for an interview. He had gone because Travis had threatened to fire him if he didn't give it a try. Called him a coward for wanting to run away. Asked how he could pretend to be an ocean racer when he couldn't face such an opportunity head-on. The man would just not let it go. So he went. Terrified and excited. Even bought a jacket and tie at Emma's suggestion, after dinner with the lady one evening and Travis had spilled the beans. That was all she said: *If you're going, give it your best. Dress nice.*

Two months after Travis's funeral, Wharton accepted him into their business program and offered Brody a rare full ride.

Which was when the nightmares began.

Not every night, but close. They all started the same. He stood at a crossroads, trapped and unable to move. Sometimes his feet were encased in concrete, sometimes he was caged, on fire, chained, whatever. All his directions were dark and threatening. And then the tide started rising. If he was lucky, he woke before the waters reached his mouth.

For the first time in his adult life, Brody spent most days in a fog. He was so exhausted from indecision, not even racing managed to lift his spirits. And that was what forced him to accept he was going.

There was no joy to the decision, nor even any real fear. His fog muted the hard moments—giving his notice just after Thanksgiving, writing Wharton, leaving the marina apartment, leaving the Outer Banks. He knew he would be back. He was also certain it would never be the same. His bonds to the Crystal Coast were splintered. From this point on, he would be just another temporary visitor.

"I remember that Christmas," Mia said. "You looked so ill."

But he was kept from the smothering emotions of those hard memories by a new realization. How those early nightmares had brought him to this point, revealing the secrets he had carried for a lifetime. It felt to Brody as if he was finally joining together the inside man to the exterior mask. There was no pleasure or relief or comfort in the act.

Reaching the point where his past connected to his now, Brody discovered he could go no further. There was so much else to tell, about multiple crises striking all together—jobs and sailing and women and life and direction. He needed a breather. He knew the confession would continue. He would reveal how lost he had become. How getting exactly what he wanted, all the goals he had set for himself, the defining reasons for life as he knew it, had proven to bring him full circle.

Before Olivia could bounce in with more questions, their mother patted his hand once, twice, as if offering Brody a silent *well done*. Then she rose to her feet and said, "I want you both to come with me."

Mia led them out of her condo and up the exterior stairs. The four buildings all faced the water, their gray facades framed in white and adorned with wide balconies and whitewashed railings. The rears were open plan, with broad passageways and staircases anchoring either end. Elevators were tucked discreetly in the northeast corners. Mia lived on the third of four floors. She climbed the side stairs and led them along the top passage that overlooked the parking area, took a set of keys from her pocket, and unlocked the door to another condo. "Son, I want you to think carefully on what I'm about to say."

Each building had three doors to a floor, set at irregular distances from one another. Brody assumed some held two bedrooms like his mother's, and others three. But this top floor held five doors, planted equidistant from one another, solid wood with brass handles and knockers. Mia stepped aside, allowing her children to enter. "You need to take time to think about your next steps."

Brody glanced at his sister. Olivia's frown was directed both at him and the empty condo. "Mom, what is this?"

"Pay attention." The keys were a separate bundle from the ones in her other pocket, those to her home and car. They jangled softly as she slipped them back in her sweater pocket. "I don't need to hear more to know you're in a hard place."

Brody had no idea what to say. The empty condo held one huge room, made larger by how the ceiling was vaulted. A trio of extensions gave the suggestion of dividers, one for the kitchen, two more splitting the bedchamber from the parlor area. He wiped his hands on his trouser legs and remained silent.

"I own this and the one next door. I never spent a penny of my salary. I didn't know if this day would ever come. But it did, and I was prepared." She gestured to the vast chamber. "I can rent this out in the high season for good money. It's how I intend to live."

Olivia started, "What on earth has Daddy done this time—?"

Mia used the rare tone that brooked neither argument nor discussion. "I won't allow any comment directed against your father. Not now, not ever. Is that clear?" When she was certain her daughter had been silenced, she went on, "These three units came with a boat slip across the street. I was going to rent that out as well. But this studio and the slip are both yours for the asking."

Mia had never been one to cling. She led them back down the stairs and over to Brody's SUV where she accepted first Olivia's and then Brody's farewell embraces. She stepped back, inspected Brody, nodded once, and said, "You've done well to grow beyond a small world defined by defeat. Do you understand what I'm saying?"

Brody had no idea how to respond.

She found nothing wrong with his silence. "The

truth is, I don't think you have any idea where your true boundaries lie." She pointed at the top floor. "If there is any chance in heaven or earth that this temporary home might help you chart your way ahead, it is yours. Consider it the Christmas gift I never thought I'd be able to offer. But this season has brought change to both our lives, and I want you to make the most of it."

8

The time with their mother silenced them both. Brody was grateful for the quiet hour. The visit had been both strange and amazingly good. His sense of carrying impossible burdens had been eased. Brody had no idea if this was a permanent change, but at some deep level he had the impression that a corner had been turned.

During the high season, afternoon traffic clogged westbound lanes leading from the beach to New Bern. Every traffic light became a parking lot. The authorities were widening 70 into four lanes all the way from Morehead to Raleigh, but the work was not yet completed, and traffic often became snarled. This time of year, however, the drive was smooth, easy, silent.

Brody felt as if his past was no longer something he strived to ignore. He had spent years slamming the door on anything other than the task at hand. He ex-

cused the act by claiming it was a necessary part of
the racing life. Single-minded focus was a key element
to winning. The same was true in Brody's professional
world. Split-second, near-instantaneous calculations
and decisions were essential. He and the traders who
acted on his information constantly raced against the
clock.

All the work, the striving, the years of competition
in two different worlds, had brought him to the point
where conversation with his mother and sister could
leave him shattered. So many of the unspoken elements that framed his life were being transformed
into—what. Brodie had no idea. Who he was, the
way ahead, remained blanketed in mist. And yet his
mother's parting words, the way Olivia sat bonded
with him in silence, suggested he was taking the right
course. For the moment, that one near certainty was
enough.

Three blocks west of the hospital, Brody turned inland and drove into Olivia's lovely neighborhood. He
stopped before an attractive two-story brick home
and cut the motor. He started to apologize, say again
how sorry he was not to have revealed himself before
this quiet December afternoon. But something held
him back. As if words alone weren't enough now and
never would be. The question was, what else could he
do to make it right?

Olivia stared at her front door and said, "Whatever it is you're facing—"

"I want to tell you. And I will. It's just—" He stopped when she turned and gave him a mother's look. Stern and unyielding. "What?"

"Let me finish."

"Okay. Sorry."

"You see this as some kind of terrible crisis. You're being hit from all sides and you don't know what to do. I get that."

Brody watched one of the girls come out the front door, wave to the car, and do a sort of bunny hop in the direction of a rope swing. He had no idea what to say.

"What if you're wrong? What if this is your chance to become who you've always wanted to be?"

"I've been wondering that exact same thing." He watched the girl start taking giant lunges, using one foot to propel herself. "The problem is, I have no idea who that is."

"Whole, Brody. A whole man. Not living from one event to the next. Not any longer." Olivia reached over and took an affectionate hold on his neck. "Finish what you've started."

"I'll try." His voice sounded strangled to his own ears.

She released him and opened her door. "I'm calling Cameron. I'm going to ask her to take you as a bona fide patient." She climbed out. "She will help. And so will I."

Brody watched the liquid-crystal fragments of a little girl bounding toward them. He wished he had the strength and wisdom to say the right thing.

Olivia started to close the door, then leaned in and said, too quietly for her daughter to hear, "Something you should know. Emma's dying. Everybody sees this except Rae, so don't you be the one to tell her. I know how much that lady has meant to you, so if you want to see Emma again, it needs to be now."

9

Rae was on close approach to Emma's home when Holden Geller finally called.

She knew a momentary urge to send him to voice-mail. Either that or answer and give the man her courtroom voice, *Not now*.

Instead, she wheeled around and headed back to her car. But not before Emma's neighbor staffing the bookstore spotted Rae and waved. She stepped under the live oak shading her car to answer, "Holden, hi."

"Rae, you don't know how many times I've started to call. But I've always been halted by simply not knowing what to say."

It felt so very good to hear the man's voice. She was tempted to finally release her tears. But Holden's tone also carried that dread note, the same indecision she had spotted in his gaze. Back on that fateful night, when she had scripted her terms in the starry night. Only now did she fully realize what had set her off.

Being in the company of a man who couldn't draw the necessary steps into proper focus. And commit. Put his future on the line. Holden's wavering attitude brought everything into a terrible ragged clarity.

"Rae?"

She was struck by a sudden memory. Age eleven, the summer she had met Curtis Gage, a tropical storm hit Atlantic Beach dead-on. This not-quite-hurricane had stripped roofs and pushed inland waters hard enough to shove any number of smaller craft over the Beaufort docks and onto dry land. It had also downed a power line directly in front of her home.

Rae had stood in her front yard, half-sheltered behind Curtis, and watched the cable hiss and writhe as it threw off a vicious stream of electric fire. To her mind, it was a living thing, a force that threatened her world. No dead element could hold such fury.

That was exactly how she felt.

"Have I lost—?"

She cut in with, "I want to apologize."

"You? Rae, for what?"

"I shouldn't have spoken to you the way I did the last time we were together. And I'm sorry that it's about to happen all over again. But today has been awful. I've spent all day arguing in court, and I lost my case. I knew going in I didn't have any chance of winning, but I held out hope for a better resolution. It didn't happen. And now I'm about to face something even worse." She paused for a breath big enough to ease the heart's ache. Then she expelled. All of it. Air and words both. "I care for you very deeply. I could so easily fall in love with you."

"Rae, I'm hearing the words, but your tone, it's saying—"

"Your job is to be quiet and pay attention. Especially since this could very well be the last conversation you and I ever have."

A heavy pause. Then, "I don't understand."

"No, you don't. But that's not the issue. Well, I suppose it is in a way." Rae spotted the neighbor stepping from the bookshop and starting toward her. The woman positively thrived on gossip. Rae chopped the air so violently the woman froze. Rae stalked over to where the oak stood between them. "Listen very carefully. I can't be with you. So long as you keep wavering, our time together is finished. You know what needs doing. Either you accept the need to move beyond your comfort zone or there's nothing further for us to discuss."

For once, Holden's tone matched her own. "Accept your terms, or else."

Rae did not give one inch. "And that is our problem in a nutshell. So long as you see them as *terms,* as an *ultimatum*, we don't have any chance of making a future together."

"That's exactly what you've done," he retorted, his voice a blade now. "Dictated next steps."

"Same answer." She both hated her tone and knew it was for the best. "I told you to listen, Holden. Not hear the words. *Listen*. Because there is a second way you could see these two conversations. That of us learning what it means to go through life as lovers and friends both, becoming a team strong enough to weather whatever comes our way. That's what I've been hoping you would take away from our last conversation. That I talked as I did, hoping to lay out steps you know in your heart are what you should do. If you would just accept the need to grow beyond where you are, realize I am helping you map out a clear path forward . . ."

She was finished. She wished for something more, something better. But just then all she could think about was how she had failed at the love thing. Again.

"Goodbye, Holden." She cut the connection, clutched the phone with both hands, and stood staring across Emma's lawn. The guest cottages formed a half circle around the back garden, lovely as wooden seashells. They fronted an emerald lawn and then a living boundary of blooming magnolia, dogwood, and coastal pine and live oak. Except what Rae saw was a gilded cage, shaped by all her wrong moves and failed loves.

She found herself mourning the life that might well never be hers. A lovely place filled with the good and the dreadful, the bliss and the pain, the everyday and the uncommon events, all knitted into a proper life because she had someone with whom it all might be shared.

If only.

As Rae entered Emma's home, she felt as if she was shifting from one existence to another. The dreary hours spent without any hint of a lifelong love belonged to someone else. The absence of a man willing to commit, a dearth of romantic options, the anger she'd felt over Holden's morose hesitation, all this had no place in Emma's home. Ever since her own mother passed, Emma had played the dual role of caring relative and island of calm. Now, though, Emma was the one who needed her to be strong. When she climbed the front steps, all her other problems simply remained in the front garden. Sulking and glum without her.

The neighbor staffing Emma's bookstore was so incensed by Rae's stiff-armed dismissal, she actually sniffed in response to Rae's quiet hello. Rae breathed the wonderful odors of books and paper and ink and stories ready to unfold. A perfume that had filled her early years and offered solace for every young wound. When she was as ready as she could be, she opened the rear door, entered the home's central corridor, and froze.

Up ahead was a man's voice. Deep and resonant and strong.

Brody's voice.

Rae remained where she was, one step inside Emma's private space. Quiet as she could, she pulled the bookstore's door shut. She was certain the voice came from Emma's bedroom, a chamber that had always been off-limits. Rae thought Brody was reading, she vaguely recognized the words, cadence, something.

The voice lifted her spirits, reignited her smile, released her chest to take a free breath. It sounded that good.

She made sure her footsteps created enough noise to alert them both. When she appeared in Emma's doorway, she became captured anew by the sight of her aunt. Smiling.

Rae pretended all was normal. She offered Brody a smile of her own. "Well, hello, stranger."

"Sorry, dear, this one's taken." Emma then told Brody, "You don't want her, anyway. She's too bony and opinionated."

Rae only half pretended at outrage. "I beg your pardon."

Brody continued to aim his smile at Rae as he replied, "It so happens I like opinions."

"They have their place, I suppose," Emma agreed,

then lifted one hand from the covers and waved in the direction of her rear garden. "Only not in here."

Rae was ready with the comeback, several in fact. But Brody's expression kept her silent, because beyond that man's smile was a whole world of emotions. Brody had brought his own burdens in here, Rae was certain of that. And something else.

She leaned against the doorway, pretending at a casual attitude. Smiled back. And studied this handsome man.

Brody's steady gaze was framed by features weathered and tanned by years of hard winds and sun. Rae felt as if she developed a snapshot that would last for years. Longer. His hair was neatly trimmed, his body strong and settled as a watchful cat. Brody met her with a steady unblinking gaze. A man this gorgeous defined danger in the romance department, as she well knew. Yet there was something else at work here. A change so deep Rae was studied a different individual. Brody's eyes held a message she would never, ever have expected to see. Not from this man.

Brody Reames was interested in more than simply hiring himself a local attorney. That much was abundantly clear.

Emma caught it, too. "How nice."

Rae felt as if her aunt's words were pulling her back from an hours-long dream. She pretended at a casual attitude and said, "Maybe I should leave and come back when I'm welcome."

"Don't be silly," Emma said. "Fetch a chair from the kitchen and join us."

For a woman whose home contained so many public spaces—library in front, guest bungalows behind—Emma had always treated her bedroom as strictly private. As she entered the kitchen and picked up her usual chair, Rae heard Brody say, "For the record, I also happen to like bones in my lady."

Rae returned down the central corridor to the amazing sound of Emma's quiet chuckle. The first in weeks. Which was why Rae drifted more than walked, carrying a hardbacked chair that had suddenly become light as a feather.

She settled the chair, then herself, and asked Brody, "What are you reading?"

"O. Henry's 'Gift of the Magi.' " Brody rolled his eyes.

"Stop that," Emma demanded. "You love it. Not as much as I do. But close."

"A guy sells his watch, a girl cuts her hair," Brody said, smiling at Rae. "So what?"

"Come closer and I'll give you what." Emma pointed at him and told Rae, "This oh-so-tough sailor lad teared up."

"It's the dust," Brody replied, still smiling at Rae. "You haven't cleaned in here for years."

A small parlor jutted off to Rae's right, formed by tall bay windows. The setting sun transformed the old glass into a multicolored shield. Rae found herself silenced by the tableau, as sad as it was beautiful. Her aunt trapped in bed, flirting with a man turned into some burnished seagoing warrior. The sun set every evening about this time. Why should this particular instant pierce her heart?

Brody lifted the book from his lap. "Should I continue?"

"Not just now. Do me a kindness and come back another day, will you?"

"Emma," Brody's breath caught, turning the woman's name into a ragged effort. "I'll be here every afternoon if you'd allow."

She studied him a long moment. "Where are you staying?"

"Atlantic Beach Doubletree."

"Why have they put your crew in a hotel?"

"They're not . . . It's a long story."

Rae expected the sort of questions she always endured when trying to avoid a topic with this woman. Instead, Emma merely said, "I positively adore long stories."

"Not this one." Brody lost his smile. "Boring and bitter both."

"Even better," Emma replied. "I've always preferred

Christmas stories that hold that flavor of some bitter spice. It fits the season's mood, at least for me."

Brody breathed, shrugged his shoulders, said merely, "Okay."

Emma said, "Two of the guesthouses are empty. Tell Doris I said to put you in six."

Brody opened his mouth, but no sound came.

"That is, if you want."

"Emma, I can't think of anything better." He hesitated, then added, "Mom has offered me a place in Oriental. But until things have been sorted out with my father, I think it's best if I decline her invitation."

"That sounds both wise and correct." This time her finger wave looked genuinely feeble. "Off with you now. I need to rest."

There was no reason on earth why seeing this man rise and bend over and kiss Emma's forehead should make Rae want to weep. Or for her eyes to burn so savagely when she stepped forward and planted her lips where Brody's had been.

Rae returned the chair, then departed by way of the rear door. She paced the front drive in slow-motion steps, doing her best to draw the world back into proper order. But when Brody finally appeared, still smiling from something the neighbor in the bookstore had told him, it was all Rae could do to wait for him to step within range.

She gripped his hand and arm and pulled him over to where the trees masked them from the house. Then Rae clutched him with all her strength, using his shirt as a way to clear her face, feeling his breath and hearing his murmured words. Not caring what he said. Brody's heartfelt tone was enough to release everything she'd carried since learning her aunt and best friend was soon to be no more.

The wind had died to nothing while they had been inside. When Rae finally released him and started down the walk, they became enveloped by a fine sea mist. Brody let her set the destination and the pace. The fog drifted slowly, casting historic Beaufort in a timeless glow. Brody had no idea where they were going, nor did he care. Rae did not lead them with a destination in mind. Whenever they reached a crossroads she stopped and waited, as if hoping the gathering dusk might whisper a direction, meaning, destination, something. Then Brody gently nudged her, and she moved forward, and they walked.

Her meandering path kept them a couple of blocks off the waterfront, away from the holiday crowds and bustling restaurants. They had the streets mostly to themselves. Occasionally a car swept by, the tires making an apologetic whisper. They passed a lovely antebellum mansion, every window alive with candles and Christmas music. A throng of people spilled onto the raised front porch. Brody smelled wood-smoke and perfume and food and booze. When Rae halted, he momentarily feared she wished to join the party. He prepared an apology, words to explain his need for a more solitary space. Then the front door opened further, illuminating Rae's features. She stared at the people in abject confusion, as if seeking to understand how they could possibly be enjoying themselves. On this, a night of impenetrable sorrow.

Gently, he wrapped one arm around Rae's shoulders and led her away. As the music and laughter dwindled to nothing, Brody assumed it was time to release his hold. But she reached up and gripped his hand, keeping him in place. They walked on, close and connected.

Brody sensed the chill working its way in, and knew it was time to find both warmth and the food Rae might not have allowed herself all day. He guided them to the Beaufort Grocery, an upscale bistro on Queen Street, and asked for a quiet indoor table. Rae seemed only partly connected to where they were and what was happening, so he ordered for them both, a single plate of the night's special—corn-fed breast of chicken stuffed with morels and served on a bed of wild rice and julienne vegetables. A glass of house white for each of them.

By the time the waiter departed, Brody knew what he wanted to say.

Rae needed something strong and heady to draw the night back into focus. Help her fit this impossible new burden into a shape she could live with. Which required linking her to the other main aspect of her life. The professional Rae. The attorney.

And besides, it was time.

He leaned across the table and said, "I want to tell you about my work."

10

"This all started in the months after World War Two," he began. "Which in terms of the trading empire's timeline, might as well have been before the last Ice Age. My first year at Wharton, I came across this guy. By that point he was reduced to a footnote in some introductory finance textbook. But back in the late forties, the man was king."

At first, Rae seemed to float there on the other side of the table. Her gaze drifted, her features remained slack. Like she was only partially recovered from some illness. Brody didn't mind. Well, he did, but not overmuch. He was fairly certain he did the right thing. If not, he had tried.

"This guy was a piece of work. Alfred Winslow Jones was middle-aged, incredibly ugly, a former communist spy." She focused on him then, a sharp glance that he rewarded with a tight smile. "Jones started by identifying underperforming companies in three industries that closely followed the overall market trends. He then bet against these firms, using the entire stock market as his bellwether. When the market fell, Jones shorted the stock of these companies, betting they would fall faster than the overall economy. The financial papers called this idea magic."

She gradually became lured into the here and now. So Brody continued, "Hedge funds sprang up almost overnight. They rode this incredible wave for over twenty years. Then the entire industry was caught out by the seventies market crash. They vanished like somebody sprayed weed killer over Wall Street."

Their food came, and eating anchored Rae further. She sipped her wine, but the level in her glass stayed more or less at the same point. Rae was watching him more intently now, listening as he went on, "When George Soros reignited hedge funds in the nineties, Alfred Winslow Jones and his fundamental ideas were ancient history. His triumphs were forgotten. I only discovered him by accident, like I said. But it seemed to me his basic concept held as much potential now as then. So, I did my thesis on modernizing the core idea. But I didn't use stocks. I expanded his concept into the biggest macro sphere possible. I went global."

Brody took a bite and waited to see if she might ask what he meant by that word, macro. When Rae merely watched and ate another minuscule forkful, he continued, "I chose three raw materials that were highly sensitive to the international economy and its overall direction. These materials also happened to be very volatile, price-wise. They formed the micro side of my algorithms."

She paused then, her glass held in midair. Brody took that as the question she did not yet care to voice, and explained, "At their most basic, algorithms are formulas into which you input data. The data alters the formula's outcome, and in my case, the outcome predicts the direction that these micro components will shift."

Rae finished everything on her plate, shook her head to his offer for a dessert or coffee, waited while he paid, then they rose and left the restaurant. She did not reconnect hands as they walked back to Emma's. But she was there with him now, listening intently as he continued, "My algorithms take full advantage of modern computational power. The goal isn't to ride the Wall Street sort of daily roller coaster. I'm after the same thing as our former spy. I want to maintain a steady course, no matter how stormy the economies and markets become. Regardless of global politics, growth, inflation, recession, whatever. And I out-performed the markets, Rae. Even so, the concept is too stable, too boring for the big New York funds.

Their fast-buck attitude to markets doesn't have room for my aims. There's no adrenaline rush here. And when they succeed, they outperform me by miles. But the risk they run is enormous."

A gentle night breeze had gathered enough force to form the mist into earthbound clouds, floating in and out of their way as they started down the block leading to Emma's home. Then his phone chimed with an incoming message. Brody was going to ignore it, but Rae spoke for the first time since leaving her aunt's bedroom. Unless of course he counted the half-formed words that had emerged with her sobs, while she clung to him so fiercely he could still feel her arms.

She said, "With everything that's happening, you should check."

Reluctantly Brody pulled out his phone, read the screen, then pocketed it before Rae could see. "It can wait."

Rae planted a warm, soft hand on the side of Brody's face. She whispered, "Thank you, friend."

Brody walked her over and held her door and stood in the headlights as she reversed from the drive and drove away. He turned and stared at Emma's silent home, wishing for a hint of solace, or the sort of comfort that the woman had offered the younger Brody during countless hard moments. But the windows were dark now. Brody touched his phone, wondering at how his boss had managed to attack in this precise moment.

The text read, My hotel, eight o'clock tomorrow. If you know what's good for you, you'll come alone.

11

The next morning Brody drove to Fortunate Harbor far more ready than he ever would have expected. This whole time, ever since being shocked awake by the lightning-streaked nightmare, Brody had known the confrontation with his boss was bound to happen. But it remained this huge amorphous question mark, dangling in the distance. Someday he would hopefully know what he wanted to do next. When that happened, and he had settled on a future direction, they would talk. Or so he had assumed.

He had no idea what shape his future should take. Only that it couldn't continue the course Jason Whitinger had set. And somehow, as he drove the almost empty beach highway, that was enough.

When he entered the hotel and passed through the lobby, Brody felt good, really good. Maybe it was just aftereffects from a genuinely earth-shattering day, confessing to Olivia, his mother's invitation, Emma,

Rae. He had thought a lot about all those things, waking early and going for a run, then packing his things and checking out. Then he'd called his mother and told her about Emma. Of course, Mia already knew about the woman's illness. Moving to Oriental did not sever decades of ties. Brody told her about the invitation, his desire to be there in case Emma needed him. Mia had replied as he'd known she would, that she'd have the place furnished in a few days, ready whenever he was.

All these experiences stayed with him. They formed the start of a new chapter. Brody had no idea where all this was headed. But so far, it all felt pretty good.

He entered the restaurant almost an hour early. Which was the norm when responding to Jacob's summons. During Brody's six years with the firm, he had seen any number of staffers in the CEO's front office, hunched over their tablets and laptops and papers, frantically prepping. Jacob Whitinger ran his company on the split-second clock and expected his team to respond "on the bounce." That was one of the man's defining trademarks, how he shouted those three words, in the office and shipboard. On the bounce.

Well, not today.

Brody ordered a house special of mashed avocado spread on a thick slice of sourdough toast, topped with two poached eggs and coriander. Fresh squeezed

OJ and coffee, black. He ate slowly, watching couples and families enjoying a pre-Christmas beachfront break. Letting his mind drift.

The previous day's three confessional bouts left him weightless, the doors to memories flung wide open. He recalled the summer he turned seventeen, still working at the marina, being invited by Jacob Whitinger to fill an empty space on his boat. That day, one of Jacob's regular crew was beached for something no one was willing to discuss. From the very first moment onboard, Brody had liked the way Jacob Whitinger handled his boat and his crew. The man's icy demeanor and dictatorial style became tempered by his genuine love of sailing and the sea. Brody admired Whitinger's ability to draw the very best from his team. He counted that three-day race as one of his finest teenage memories. Right up there with the months he'd spent in Rae's company.

When Brody neared graduation from Wharton, he submitted his application to Jacob Whitinger personally. His other job interviews were little more than placeholders. Jacob invited him down, gave Brody a surgeon's exam, then set the terms and conditions. Take it or leave it. When Brody accepted, Jacob offered a final warning. Either Brody proved himself in the firm and on the water, or he was beached. Brody knew the man spoke ice-cold truth. Until recently, he had remained relatively content just making the grade.

He was lingering over a second cup of coffee when his phone pinged. The text read, Suite 305. Five minutes.

Brody actually said the words aloud. "Not today."

He typed in a reply, wondering at his first-ever calm. I'm in the restaurant if you'd like to meet.

He turned off his phone. Brody watched the light strengthen beyond the restaurant's east-facing windows, and wondered if the other patrons could sense the coming explosion.

Jacob Whitinger arrived wearing his sailing gear, clearly intending to show Brody exactly what was at stake. This wasn't just about a job. His career as an ocean racer was on the line.

Whitinger gave the approaching waiter a smile that fooled neither the guy nor Brody. The waiter was already backing away when Jacob said he didn't want anything. Jacob seated himself and inspected Brody with eyes the color of glacier ice, old and cold. Brody knew the man was sixty-eight, but he could easily have been ten years younger. Extremely fit, perfectly groomed even when preparing for a day on the open waters. Stationed in his chair like a predator ready to pounce. Attack. Devour.

Brody knew Jacob was furious over having to come downstairs. Effectively summoned by one of his crew. He hid it fairly well, but the tells were visible. Tells were a sailor's means of racing ahead of competitors. Little cat's-paw indentations in open waters, showing where sudden wind-bursts from a new direction offered a chance to pull ahead—or be demolished by the opposition. Jacob's tells were tiny indentations carved to either side of his eyes, and a tight strip of red by his temples.

His voice was an assassin's melody. "You know what your problem is?"

Brody found it strange that he still had no idea how he wanted this confrontation to play out. He simply wasn't as prepared as he should be. Just the same, he had never felt this immune to Jacob's fury. As if his utter lack of preparation was actually a good thing. The total illogicality of his position left him almost giddy.

Jacob told him, "You don't love winning enough. Sure, you like it. But you don't live for it." His boss shifted forward a trace, readying for the strike. "Which means you'll always be second mate. Or worse, second rate."

Brody felt the response drift in through the open terrace doors, lofted by sunlight and the ocean's heady tang. "Why were you so angry over my speaking at the conference?"

Jacob's gaze sparked, a hint of the molten interior revealed. There and gone. "You stepped out of bounds. You should have asked permission. And you know it."

"I think something else is at work. My speech and the reception I gained, all that challenged the box you want to keep me in."

His challenge was all it took. Jacob's quiet snarl was enough to turn heads at all the surrounding tables. "You need me more than you'll ever know. I'm the guy on the front line. I'm the winner you'll never be. I give you more than a boat and a job. I give you a *purpose*. That's something you'll *never* find on your own."

As Jacob rose to his feet, he realized the attention now cast their way. The effort required to restore his meaningless smile was huge. "Now you hide behind that woman's skirts because you don't have what it takes to meet me head on. And you never will."

This from a man with a dozen attorneys on his payroll. "Here's what's going to happen," Brody said. "You're going to offer me two contracts. One for my work, and one for my sailing gig. That's the way it has to be from now—"

"You don't dictate terms." He thumped his fist on the linen-draped table. "Not now, not ever."

Brody ignored him. "And you're going to pay me the bonus I've earned. This year and last."

Jacob actually laughed. "Or what, you walk?"

"No, Jacob. Because I already have. Either you lure me back with a proper—"

Jacob leaned in so close Brody smelled the man's aftershave. "Here's my counteroffer. You crawl back and beg for another chance. Or you'll never race on any boat ever again. I'll see to that personally. You mark my words."

Brody sat and watched the champion racer storm from the room. He felt the diners' attention turn his way and didn't care. There was a unique satisfaction in lifting his coffee cup and finding his hand was still steady, despite the lingering cinders and smoke Jacob had left in his wake.

Brody remained seated, facing the strengthening day, for over an hour. When he finally signaled the waiter for his bill, he had formulated what he thought were two key questions designed to carry him forward.

The lobby's Christmas tree blinked a cheery farewell as he departed. He crossed the parking lot, climbed into his ride, started the engine, rolled down all the windows, and sat staring into the day ahead. Coming to terms with this new compass heading.

Question one was, why did losing his chance to race feel so meaningless? He knew Jacob Whitinger was as good as his threat.

The answer was, the joy that had once defined his

sailing life was gone. He had to find a new way forward.

Which led straight to question two.

What now?

As if in response, his phone chimed.

When Brody checked the screen, he realized it was not an incoming message but rather a reminder that it was time to call Cameron, the therapist.

The very instant she came on the line, Cameron demanded, "Are you prepared to discuss the concept of real change?"

"I've given it a lot of thought," Brody replied. "I'll talk about that if you insist. But I'd really like to spend this time on something else."

Cameron hesitated, then said, "I'm listening."

Brody felt as though he'd prepped for days. Which, in truth, he might have. The morning's tight calm remained as he recounted the exchange with his boss.

Amazing.

Brody finished with, "It was only after Jacob left that I realized how much he sounded like my dad. This was the first time he's revealed that hidden edge. But I've seen hints for years. Everybody who works for Jacob knows it's part of him."

"You came face-to-face with the man's dark side."

"Yes, but that's not . . ." Brody took a breath. Stared out the side window. Going over what had just taken place. "I feel like I've spent years running from my father. All this time, all this effort, trying to carve out a different life. A better world to call my own. And what happens? There, in my boss, I discover the same things I've been determined to leave behind." Brody traced a palm's shadows on his side window, like he was reading a hidden script. "You know that saying, *You can't go home again*? What a joke. I can't leave home behind."

"May I say something?"

"Absolutely. I'm done."

"Your sister and Rae both called this morning and said I should accept that you are genuinely ready for therapy. They think I should take you at your word and accept you as a bona fide patient."

Brody was glad the woman's voice came through the car's speakers, and he wasn't seated where she could see how the news stabbed him. Despite years filled with countless mistakes, look how they responded.

As if they were his friends. And cared about him. Despite everything.

"Tell me something about your father," Cameron said. "The first thing that comes to mind."

He cleared his throat best he could and launched in. "There was a sign on the wall by the front door that read, 'My roof, my rules.' That pretty much says everything you need to know about our home. Memories of my father . . . I could never measure up. Everything he said, the way he watched me, it all came down to how I was a walking disgrace. A constant disappointment. Pop was permanently angry with me. He was certain I'd never amount to anything."

Brody heard the flat tone, the utterly calm way he spoke, like he was listening to someone else. He never talked about his father. And yet, here he was, revealing the hurts that had defined his early years. But all he could think of was how his former boss had glared at him. The same cold fury. The same bitter disdain.

Cameron said, "I am going to speak with you as a clinician. It's important you pay careful attention. What I have to tell you will frame the coming sessions. And this should assist you in confronting the tumult of emotions that are bound to arise."

But he didn't feel any tumult. Brody could not have been any calmer if he stopped breathing. Just the same, he said, "I understand."

"It makes perfect sense that you have found yourself close to someone so similar to your father. We seek familiarity and consistency in our relationships."

Jacob Whitinger might as well have been seated there beside him, shaped by sunlight and the rage he had revealed. Brody replied, "Whatever consistency there was in my relationship with my father was bad. Awful. I thought I'd fled in every possible way."

"That changes nothing. Your childhood state, this fundamental anxiety, resulted from a desperate need to connect. You sought a means to accommodate your father's demands and expectations." Cameron's voice was a calm anchor holding him steady against the invasion. She spoke in a detached manner, but to Brody's mind she might as well have sung the words. "This concept forms a core tenet of what is known as the attachment theory. Tell me something, Brody. Thinking of your father, what is the first emotion that comes to your mind?"

The two men, his father and Jacob Whitinger, formed luminous impressions inside Brody's ride. He replied, "I feel guilty. I couldn't be the son he wanted. It was all my fault."

"This is a very normal response. At the time, in your childhood era, feelings of guilt validated the defenses you developed to survive life with your father."

Brody shifted in his seat, inspecting the rage that had formed the common denominator to any wrong move. "And now? I'm talking about coming full circle, and meeting the same awful situation with my boss."

Cameron hesitated, then replied, "These issues define you because until this point you have never been ready to confront them. Your shame arises naturally from this fractured relationship with your father. You were left feeling inherently flawed. So, you hid yourself. You tried to remain invisible so you could avoid feeling further shame, so he would not hurt and denigrate you even more than he already did."

Brody recalled the hours and days he had spent doing his best for Jacob's company and the man's sailing crew. Holding to a quietly cheerful tone, utterly disconnected from the wrath that was occasionally unleashed. His job was to remain the quiet observer. Hiding in plain sight. For years.

Cameron continued, "When fight or flight doesn't work or isn't possible, a child hunkers down and does their best to go unnoticed." She paused, but to Brody it was as though the day carried a drumbeat of soft confrontation. "This has a secondary effect, one that has defined another part of your life and world. It has rendered you unable to have genuine feelings in a relationship."

Other half-seen faces gradually took shape, a crowd of women whose names he could not recall, as Cameron continued, "Your father was not emotionally accessible. He was not there for you. So, you developed a shield against this constant threat of more pain and disappointment."

He coughed because it was the only way to force out the air necessary to ask, "Why am I only seeing this now?"

"Because now you are ready. You now have the strength and maturity to accept why you hurt so many women in your life." She paused then, just long enough for the car to echo with what she did not say. Then she went on, "This shield kept you intact so that you and I could arrive at this point. Preparing to redefine a new perspective on life."

He said the words because he needed to. Though they bit like acid. "And love."

"Exactly. So let me leave you now with one question. It still comes back to the issue of defining real change. But as you said, the concept is too large. So, tell me this. What one element of personal change do you want to consider next?"

His crowd of past pressures and errors vanished. In their place, a few words became shaped by the daylight and the now empty vehicle.

Brody replied, "I want to understand the meaning of one word. *Home*."

12

Rae felt surprisingly happy as she entered her office the next morning. Over coffee, she had called Cameron and related some of how Brody had acted the previous night. Enough to explain why Rae thought Cameron should take Brody's desire for therapy as both real and valid. The conversation left her feeling almost weightless. As if she had sent Brody an unexpected Christmas gift.

Lana was in a Friday state of mind, earpods in place as she worked her computer, bouncing slightly and humming to a melody Rae did not recognize. When Rae's shadow fell on the desk, Lana pulled out one pod and said, "Can't help but love the Black Eyed Peas."

"I'll take your word for it."

"Brody Reames called. Something's come up and he urgently needs to meet. Your morning was pretty free, so I've booked him in first."

"Good. You just saved me a phone call."

"Yeah, I kinda figured you wouldn't mind another dose of that guy. And Amiya has called twice. She says to tell you she is growing angrier with every passing minute." Lana offered an impish grin. "I love how that lady sings her words even when she's mad."

Amiya was one of Rae's closest friends, and a lady with every reason to be angry. Rae asked, "What's got you so happy?"

"My folks collected the kids for the weekend," Lana replied. "Soon as I'm done here, Carl and I are heading out. I forget where. Doesn't matter. Away is enough."

"Go now."

Lana's normally bright nature became incandescent. "Really?"

"Absolutely." Rae flipped through her phone calendar. "I've got Brody in an hour, the Dixons after lunch, the rest of the day is your basic catch-up on all the paperwork I haven't accomplished this week."

"You sure you won't wither and die without me?" The concern was turned mocking by how she had already gathered up her jacket and purse, stowed her pods and iPlayer, and was heading out. "Say the word and I'm happy to—" The closing door cut off whatever fake offer she'd been shaping.

The resulting silence was, Rae decided, just what the doctor ordered. She left her office door open so she could watch for new arrivals. She rounded her desk, settled in her chair, and just sat there. Feeling almost content. It was such a rare sensation, she took time to try and give it a name, if not a reason.

Hard as it was to admit, it all came down to Brody. The guy she had always assumed was as close to heartless as a man could come, he was the one who caught her when she fell. And did so with the care and concern of, well . . .

She might as well go ahead and say it.

Last night he had held her with a lover's gentle strength.

Rae watched dust motes do their ballerina dance in the sunlight and wondered at the changes contained in this admission. Brody Reames. The man who looked at her with a special light in his gaze. The man who knew what she needed and gave with a totality that left her, well . . .

Weightless.

Rae rose from her chair and walked to the corner kitchenette in Lana's office. She poured and doctored a mug of coffee, returned to her desk, and picked up her phone. What this moment called for was a friend who might help her put this item in proper perspective. Maybe.

The only reason why Rae's relationship with Amiya Morais wasn't comical was that they loved each other like sisters. Amiya was daughter to the retired chief executive of the Fortunate Harbor's parent company. She now voted his stock and held his seat on the board. Which effectively meant Amiya was also Rae's biggest client. Along with her fiancé, who served as president of their North American operations.

But wait, there's more.

This fiancé happened to be none other than Curtis Gage. The man who had been Rae's very own first true love. The same man who broke her young heart.

Which under any other circumstances would have defined uncomfortable. But with Amiya and Curtis, it simply bound them more tightly together. Friends for life.

Amiya answered the phone with, "Why was I forced to learn about Emma's health through my father?"

"That's an easy one," Rae replied.

"I'm listening."

"I've got too much going on just now to totally break down and sob."

A quiet moment, then, "All right. I accept that as at least partly valid."

"Anyway, it didn't work. Last night it finally hit me, and I totally lost it."

"Oh, Rae."

"In front of a new client, no less. Just collapsed into his arms and bawled."

Amiya replied, "I should probably not be smiling."

"I'm not nearly done." Rae was enjoying herself now, despite everything. No one on earth could get her going quite like Amiya. "This particular client is also a former flame."

"Now you're joking."

"A while after Curtis and I broke up, Brody arrived on the scene." She leaned back in her chair, stared at the ceiling, and remembered. "He was just exactly what I needed at the time."

"Are we talking new love?"

"Hardly. Love was the last thing I wanted. More like, a double dose of salsa."

"So . . . Handsome?"

"Think buccaneer with dimples."

Amiya laughed out loud. "How long has it been?"

"Eight years, give or take."

"Who broke things off?"

"It wasn't like that," Rae replied. "Brody left for the autumn racing circuit, and a week or so later, I went back for my senior year at university."

"Racing?"

"He's been a fanatic sailor since forever. He's also

Morehead City born and raised. I've seen him around every now and then. We've stayed on good but distant terms."

"Now he shows up, asks you to represent him, and you just leap into his arms?"

"Not exactly. First, he asked for an appointment, and we talked shop. Then yesterday, I walked into Emma's and he was sitting by her bed, reading to her." Rae's smile crimped at the edges. "She looked genuinely happy for the first time since forever. Emma invited him to move in to one of her cottages."

Amiya's laughter was bell-like. "Does Santa have something special to put under your tree?"

"I wish I knew."

"Girl, for real?"

"It gets worse. You remember Holden?"

"The man who helped save our company? Puleese."

"He's made his intentions clear in the romance department. Sort of."

That silenced Amiya.

Rae offered a shortened version of the two most recent less-than-perfect exchanges with the man interested in, well, bonding. She finished with, "The simple truth is, I don't think Holden is ready to commit to the sort of relationship I'm after."

"Which is?"

"Fifty-fifty. With no secrets on the professional front."

Amiya's smile was still there in her voice, shimmering in the December daylight. "You did right."

"I wish I could be so sure."

"Rae, listen to me. This sounds better than good, what you've done, and what it represents."

"I can't tell you what it means, hearing you say that."

"Maybe you should have it tattooed on your forearm. The next time Holden starts pressing, you roll back your sleeve and show him just how permanently serious you are when it comes to the fifty-fifty arrangement."

"Okay, number one, I'm not into body ink. And second, I'm not sure there will be another time."

Rae half expected Amiya to offer advice, assurance, maybe even say she should insert herself into the equation. Instead, she asked, "What about this buccaneer?"

She was about to say that even thinking about a future with Brody left her queasy, when her personal phone rang. "I have to go. Emma's on the other line."

"Rae, wait. I'm coming down late tonight for a quick visit with Daddy. Can I go see her?"

"Of course. She'll love that." She hit the other phone, told Emma, "Hang on just a second." Then back to Amiya with, "Are you staying through Christmas?"

"I want to, but we'll see. Curtis is due back today from his regular battle with the Delhi board. He's meeting me at Daddy's. Everything depends on what he won't discuss by phone."

"See you tomorrow," Rae promised, then switched phones and asked, "What's the matter?"

"What an utterly dreadful way to say good morning," Emma replied. "Nothing's wrong."

"Really?"

"Child, yes. I'm feeling much better today. Which is why I'm calling. Will you do something for me?"

"Is that a joke?" Rae could hear the lift to her voice, like a weight had up and floated away. "Yes, Emma. Anything."

"I'm scheduled for another exam. Now that I'm feeling better, I don't want that doctor coming anywhere near my house."

"I've met Dr. Asher, and I couldn't agree more."

"The warmth of his bedside manner approaches absolute zero," Emma said.

"I hope you told him."

"Twice. It was like bouncing rocks off a bullet-proof vest."

"When is your appointment?"

"Four, this afternoon."

"I'll be there."

"Bring your gentleman friend. I may need help with the maneuvers."

Rae started to offer the knee-jerk response, how Brody was a client, nothing more. But the day was too fine for myths. "No problem."

"Thank you, dear. But that's not why I wanted to speak with you. Well, it is. But not really."

"You've lost me."

There was no reason why Emma's request would offer her heart such wings. None at all.

Brody entered while she was still on the phone with Emma. He returned her wave through the open office doorway, then planted himself in front of her painting. For such a strong and handsome man, Rae thought he possessed a fragile air. Something she could definitely understand.

As Rae cut the connection, Brody offered the painting a solemn nod. She found that oddly moving. Rae had loved the artwork from her very first viewing. A couple in art deco finery danced along the seashore, accompanied by a few other distant pairs. The idiotically romantic scene spoke to her of love's impossible moments, the rapture of taking time for the splendid grandeur of affection. No matter what.

As she entered Lana's office, something about his expression had her wondering if perhaps Brody wished himself into the scene. Rae focused on the print and tried to recall the last time she'd observed it with anything other than bitter regret.

Brody said, "You called Cameron. About me."

"First thing this morning," Rae confirmed.

"I can't tell you what it means, you and Olivia asking her to become my therapist." He still had not looked her way. "After everything I've done, all the wrong moves . . ." He took a long breath. "Thank you, Rae."

They might have stood there for hours, sharing the unspoken. But there simply wasn't time. "You needed to speak with me about something?"

"I do, yes. Shepphard Creighton, head of the Creighton Fund. He texted and requested a conference call."

"Is that really his name?"

"Yes. A viscount, no less. He jokes about how it took six generations to lose everything except his silly title."

"So, he's British."

"He is, but minus the stuffiness. His fund is based in Atlanta. The biggest in the southeast by some measurements. Jacob despises him. We've met a couple of times at conferences. He's actually a nice guy, by all accounts." Just the same, talking about this man elevated Brody's tension to where Rae could almost count the stress lines. "I think he wants to offer me a job."

"When is this supposed to take place?"

"Eleven."

She glanced at her watch. Plenty of time to slot that in. "You want me to handle it, correct?"

"Rae, yes, absolutely."

"Fine." Rae touched his arm, trying to calm him. She thought it was like settling a nervous horse. "There's something I need *you* to do."

13

They left her office five minutes later. Brody suggested they take his double-cab, so there would be extra room for whatever. Soon as they were underway, Rae settled against the side door so she could watch the man driving. Brody wore a wool knit cap, thin and drawn tight to his head. It highlighted his face's strong lines, the pronounced cheekbones, the chill to his glacial-blue eyes. Brody must have felt her eyes, because he glanced over and smiled. "What?"

"Thank you for doing this."

"You kidding? Emma was one lady I could always rely on. Hard as things got, she was always ready with a plate of those amazing cookies and that awful tea." He rolled down both windows on his side. "A month or so before my uncle offered me the weekend gig, things were pretty bad around the house. I was already hooked on math and sailing both, which meant running away wasn't really an option. I asked

Emma if I could move into one of her little cabins, pay my keep by doing whatever was needed around the place."

She wrapped her jacket in tighter, fighting off the chill of highway driving with both windows down. "I never knew that."

"You want me to roll up the windows?"

"Never."

He pointed to the glove compartment. "There's another cap in there. Always keep a fresh one for coming off the water." He smiled at the sight of her fitting it in place. "Only Rae Alden could make a sailor's knit cap look beautiful."

She had no idea how to respond to his compliment, so she asked, "What did Emma say?"

"That I needed to stand tall and remain confident things were going to work out."

"That sounds just like her."

"Then she told me about sea glass."

Rae felt her jaw drop open. "No way."

Brody glanced over. "Not you, too."

"I thought I was the only one."

He slowed so as to give her a longer look. "So did I."

"Tell me what she said." It wasn't that Rae suspected him of telling tales. More like, she needed to know how deep this connection went.

"Sea glass was her favorite gemstone. When I told

her it was just glass, she swatted my head and told me to pay attention." Brody was watching the road now, or rather, staring ahead and smiling at the unseen. "The sea took little bits of the broken and changed them."

Rae was nodding now. She was hearing Emma's exact words coming alive again, right here in Brody's ride. She could no longer see the man driving, nor did it matter. He spoke, and she heard a different voice.

"Years and years of polishing and smoothing, turning these tiny fragments into the most beautiful jewels on earth. Gifts from the sea and the sunlight and the passage of hard times."

Rae liked how this man she thought she knew needed to release one hand from the wheel and wipe his face. She could not get over how it felt for the two of them to be so impacted by the same memory.

Brody went on, "I always suspected she had a word with my Uncle Travis. Soon after that conversation, he offered me the place to stay. I never spoke with Emma about it, though. Too worried I might jinx things."

"Your parents never asked where you spent your weekends?"

"My mother gave it her blessing, she and Travis were tight." His face grew new lines. "I never heard word one from Dad. He might have been glad to see me gone."

The wind sang a stronger melody now, so potent Rae heard herself say, "My mother died on Christmas Eve when I was nine years old. My father passed eleven days later. He'd had cancer of some kind, it'd spread everywhere. Mom was a severe diabetic, and caring for him put too much strain on her already weak system."

"Rae, I'm so sorry, I never knew."

"They were incredibly in love. That's the most enduring memory I have, how they cared for each other. Despite everything. I moved in with Emma on Christmas Day. Daddy was already in hospice care. Emma's husband, my uncle Al, had died that spring. Emma called me the very best Christmas gift ever. For all the wrong reasons."

She liked even more how Brody's voice sounded almost cracked around the edges when he said, "That sounds so much like her."

"I had my bad days at first. Emma liked to pretend they didn't happen, or at least didn't matter. 'Mere aberrations,' she called them. She said I was a perfect example of a female clock who missed half a second once each year."

Brody wiped his face a second time. The sight was rimmed by little crystalline elements now, especially when Rae needed to do the same.

"Then I turned twelve, and it all came crashing in. I entered a new school that autumn and hated every minute. I felt like everywhere I looked, I was brought back to the same terrible truths. All that death and loss. Both parents. Uncle Al."

Brody managed, "Your whole world, and all you had left was one sick lady."

Rae used both hands this time. It was suddenly very important to see him clearly. She wasn't used to people understanding her so profoundly. Like Brodie shared her thoughts as well as her words. "Emma put up with me for an entire autumn. Then she borrowed a boat from Travis and took me to Cape Lookout. She told me we were going to stay out there until I found her a decent piece of sea glass. Even if it took all winter, we weren't going—"

That was as far as she got.

Brody slowed and put on his blinker and pulled into a parking lot that had been emptied by winter. He reached across the central divide. It felt beyond natural to lean into his embrace. Beyond good.

She waited until she had things back under control. Then, "We need to be going."

He was not letting go. He just held on. His face nestled where her hair emerged from the cap and spilled over her neck. She could feel his breath. Steady. Strong.

Rae wanted to stay where she was. She wanted, she wanted . . .

She gently pushed him away, settled back into the seat, waited as Brody put the truck into drive and turned onto the highway. Then she finished, "I've apologized to her so many times. Emma claims it's the second finest Christmas she's ever had."

Those were the last words either of them spoke until they pulled into the marina's main lot. He watched the masts tilt and sway, giving her time to collect herself. Then he reached for her hand and held it a long time. Twice he opened his mouth, ready to speak, but remained silent.

Rae put her free hand on top of his. She used both hands to squeeze his fingers. Hard as she could. Silence had never felt so sweet. Or so right.

Brody had parked where they could sit and watch the Island Marina in holiday season. Rae liked how he was willing to wait for her guidance. More than that. It touched her at a very deep level, this man's gift of trust.

"Pretend Jacob is watching. You're still open to a counteroffer?" Rae pretended to ignore how Brody's entire body tensed at the man's name. "Because if I was in his place, furious over how you're being pursued by another group . . . You say he doesn't like this Lord Viscount?"

"They loathe each other."

"Given what you've told me, Jacob is boiling. So, he'll ask one of your crew mates—"

"He doesn't ask. Jacob orders."

"Somebody is checking the marinas. Seeing what you've been up to."

Brody glanced over. "What am I up to, Rae?"

She told herself it was silly to be moved by how Brody showed her such openhanded trust. "What would you most like to see happen?" When he remained silent, she went on, "I'm not talking about just today. If you could name one thing—"

"Jacob accused me of not being a true competitor. Somebody who's driven to win. Who takes losing like a sword to the gut. He uses that expression all the time. A challenge to his crew."

"When did he tell you this?"

"Earlier this morning."

"Brody, you met Jacob Whitinger alone? Without telling me?"

He shifted in his seat. Grave now. "I needed to do this, Rae. Look him in the eye. Alone. And tell him I wasn't dancing to his tune anymore."

She found herself unable to argue with that. "Will you tell me what happened?"

Brody related their confrontation in the Fortunate Harbor restaurant. Rae found herself reflecting on how she now viewed Brody Reames, the young professional.

Despite the tense exchange, Jacob's rage and vindictive nature on full display, Brody's account was calmly analytical. Then he segued smoothly into his conversation with Cameron.

Stripping himself bare in the process.

Brody finished with, "Back to your question."

For a brief instant, Rae had no idea what he was talking about. "Okay."

"Before a major storm comes onshore, the air crackles with an energy, a pressure. You know a major change is on the way. That's how it felt after Jacob left. Like everything that's been happening over the past months became perfectly clear. The tempest has struck. Jacob is only a small part of it. Maybe the most visible, but worrying about him is like being blinded by a lightning strike and ignoring the whole storm."

Rae felt her chest expanding. Like she needed more space to absorb everything that was pouring in. She tried to tell herself she was focused on a client's needs. But she had never been one for lying to herself. Even here. When his confession felt like it stripped her bare.

Brody said, "What if it's time to give up racing?"

A tremor ran through her bones. Crazy. Especially since she could not say why. "Not because of Jacob."

"No. What if it's time to love sailing for sailing's

sake?" His eyes were blue-gray crystal globes. Wonderous. Matching his tone. "What if I strip away the competition and stress and sacrifices . . . Rae, I don't know what to fit inside that hole."

She could almost read the words there in his open gaze. "You're making room for something else."

He just looked at her.

"A different life," she said, breathless now. "One with a greater sense of balance."

Brody struggled to repeat that word. Like he was learning a new language, one that required him to fashion a new sound. A new structure. *Balance.*

She went on, "Step away from an existence where ocean racing is the focal point. Energy, time, the best of who you are, right now it goes there first."

His response emerged slowly, like he was forced to pull the words out one by one. "I've never seen it like that before. But it's true. I never . . ."

For Rae, the entire morning took on an uncanny quality. Everything she thought she knew about Brody Reames belonged to a different era. "You're searching for a way through a transition. And right now, you have no idea what shape that's going to take."

His gaze was an open door. "None."

She nodded slowly. There was so much more to say. But now was not the time. Except for two simple words. "I understand."

Brody searched for the right way ahead. He was desperate for her to help. He wanted her to assist in this exploration of life's new dimensions. She could see it in how he watched her, how he had held her when she was weakest, how he'd revealed his most dreaded secrets.

Trusted her fully.

"You do, don't you. Understand."

"Yes." She tapped the console's central clock. "It's time to make the call."

"My name is Rae Alden, attorney at law. I'm calling in reference to your interest in Brody Reames."

Shepphard Creighton asked, "You represent him?"

"I do."

"In what capacity?"

"I serve as his attorney of record. Excuse me, but should I call you 'my lord'?"

"Certainly not. Am I correct in assuming Mr. Reames takes my offer seriously?"

"That might be presuming too much, Mr. Creighton. As there is no formal offer on the table."

"Indeed, not. I stand corrected. And please call me Shep."

His speech was a remarkable blend of upper-crust English and Atlanta honey. Rae found herself charmed. Which was a risk. "Again, sir, premature."

His laugh sounded through Brody's truck. Rae thought it was genuine. She glanced at Brody. He remained stationary, turned slightly so as to be fixated on her. He showed her the most remarkable expression, so gentle, so trusting. Rae was tempted to mute the phone and ask if he was actually listening to the conversation. But Shep, the Viscount, chose that moment to ask, "How shall we proceed?"

"You requested the call, sir."

"So I did. So I did." He cleared his throat. "Well, to the matter at hand. I was utterly taken by your client's recent presentation. Which electrified the conference, I must say. He was all anyone spoke about. Allies in Charlotte related to me what happened next. I assume Mr. Reames has mentioned the furious tirade that greeted your client upon his return to Jacob Whitinger's place of business."

Rae decided not to respond.

Shep continued, "By all accounts, poor Jacob was livid to discover his hidden asset had now been revealed to the greater world. So I had my team pull together all Mr. Reames's journal articles."

This was new. "How many did they locate?"

"Five. Please tell me that's all there are, else I'll be forced to dismiss a favorite researcher."

When Brody offered a slow nod, Rae replied, "Five is correct."

"They made quite a fascinating read, I must tell

you. Excellent work, start to finish, a true astonishment. I was sorely disappointed I had not heard of Mr. Reames before then."

Rae studied this buccaneer seated beside her, this man with his remarkable mind. She found herself relishing this opportunity to hear another man's praise. "Tell me why Mr. Reames holds such interest to your group."

"Can he hear us?"

"He can."

"My company's focus is the management of family savings. Some very large, but a considerable portion of our clients are simply preparing for the future. College educations, retirements, vacation homes, and such. We don't do showy. We specialize in building a solid financial footing over years. Decades. Sometimes generations. What Mr. Reames has accomplished opens an entirely new arena. We, our clients, can use his work as a means of diversification. His aim is precisely the same as ours. Steady long-term returns."

"Nothing flashy."

"What works for Wall Street is an anathema to us and our clients," Creighton agreed. "No roller coasters, no skyrockets. Steady, calm, safe passage through our turbulent and risky economic times."

Rae searched for some reaction, a signal, but all Brody showed her was that same watchful calm.

Trusting her. With everything.

Rae said, "I suppose that brings us to the point."

"Indeed." Again, Creighton cleared his throat. "I do hope you will spare us both unnecessary regret and take me at my word. When it comes to members of my firm, I do not negotiate. I offer what I feel is top dollar. I expect nothing less in return. Is that clear?"

Rae continued to meet Brody's gaze. "I'm listening."

Creighton named a sum. "Plus bonus, of course."

The amount completely shattered Brody's calm. She could see he was about to speak, agree, object it was too much, something totally absurd. So, she did the only thing she could think of. Rae reached across the divide and pressed a finger to his lips. She said, "There is one final issue we need to cover before my client and I can consider your proposal."

"I'm listening."

Rae leaned back and said what she had been thinking of since hearing of this man with the silly name. "One of the elements that makes Brody Reames unique is his passion for open waters."

"I will not, under any circumstances, allow him to continue racing on that scoundrel's team."

Rae thought Brody's own words fit perfectly. "What if he was to give up racing entirely?"

The phone went silent.

"If Brody, Mr. Reames, is starting on this new course with your group, perhaps now is the time to enjoy sailing for sailing's sake." Rae gave that a moment. "You probably expected him to demand specific periods away, timed to the racing calendar. Added to that would be training with his crew. What does that total, two months each year? More?"

"I confess this prospect almost kept me from reaching out." His words slowed considerably. "What would you suggest?"

Rae found it absurd, how her heart decided this was the moment to flip into overdrive. "You allow him time each month to work off site."

Creighton demanded, "Where would he be based?"

"The Outer Banks. Specifically, the region around Beaufort."

A long silence, then: "Ten days each month. Timed to a somewhat flexible calendar, dependent upon office schedules."

"Thank you very much, sir. In that case, I believe we have arrived at an offer my client will find acceptable."

"When can I have his response? More importantly, when can he start?"

"I will discuss both matters with him, and respond before the close of business day after tomorrow. Unless you'd prefer to wait until after the holidays?"

"Certainly not."

"Until then." She cut the connection and watched as Brody's hands reached over and took full hold.

She spent a timeless moment reveling in the man's strength and warmth and closeness. The she gently freed herself and said, "Let's go shopping."

14

As they rose from the car, Brody saw the marina's manager enter into discussion with another customer. He and Rae settled where the marina's central building blocked the wind. Brody had only been back a couple of times. In the early years after he left for university, the place was too full of his uncle's absence. By the time he settled into Charlotte and his new roles as analyst and sailing master on Jacob's boat, the Island Marina was just part of the life Brody had walked away from.

The marina held a happy lived-in atmosphere and smelled of wet canvas and fuel and fishing gear and salt. In the months after Brody bade the Outer Banks a bitter farewell, his finest and hardest dreams always started with a whiff of that sea-laden perfume.

Charlie Trafford, the marina's manager for the past decade, glanced over long enough to show Brody wide eyes and an upraised finger. Brody waved back, then led Rae over to where the dockside walkway joined with the structure's waterfront veranda. He heard Rae ask, "A doubloon for your thoughts."

"I was remembering the last time Uncle Travis and I spoke."

Rae settled her left hand next to his, just barely touching. But close enough for him to feel her warmth spread through his entire frame. She asked, "Will you tell me?"

Her closeness only made the recollection more vivid. "It was a day or so before I left for school. Travis was really sick, everything about him looked like he was melting. But whenever I asked, he always said it was just a bad chest cold. I should have, you know . . ."

Her hand shifted over so as to rest gently on top of his. "This isn't about regrets. Besides, if Travis wanted you to worry, he'd have said something different. Right?" When Brody did not respond, she squeezed. "Tell me what he said."

The words sang in the chill December breeze. "He told me my fears were all based on a myth. I thought staying here meant keeping hold of everything that made this one day so special. What I didn't understand was how I was caught up in this glorious tidal pool. Beautiful, easy, floating and spinning, and loving every minute. But sooner or later the tides would change and the pool would be flooded, and my life would never be the same. And down deep, I already knew this."

He was silenced by Rae stepping away and shaking her head and brushing the windswept hair from her face. Brody thought she cleared her cheeks as well, but he couldn't be certain. Then she pointed and said, "Here he comes."

Charlie Trafford was the other face of island life, a gray-haired castaway with the air of a cheerful cynic. His nose was heavily veined, his eyes red-rimmed and stained yellow. But he knew boats, and he was an excellent judge of people. And he was honest. Charlie liked to say he needed to love money a lot more than he did to steal. Brody thought the marina's owners had chosen well.

Charlie stumped over and made a noisy process of welcoming Brody. Talking about old times, how much Charlie missed Brody's uncle. He welcomed Rae with the warmth of a natural salesman. The marina was moving at a holiday pace. A few people smiled in their direction, but mostly they got on with preparing for a day on the water. Charlie dealt with any number of issues while he chatted, keeping a steady eye on his three dockhands as they filled chests with ice, pumped gas, handled a few rentals, brought him papers to check and sign.

Mostly, Brody drifted. The wind might as well have blown straight through him. The only thing keeping him firmly tethered to earth was Rae's hand.

Finally, Rae said, "We need to accelerate."

Brody told Charlie, "I'm interested in buying a boat. Ocean going. Thirty feet plus."

Charlie's gaze took on a keener slant. "Price?"

Brody shook his head. "First, let's see if there's anything worth considering."

"Well, sure, we've got some fine craft here." Charlie led them down the last quai holding the longer-term berths. He halted before a trio of weary craft, all of them over twenty years old and severely weathered. Three couples appeared on the marina café's rear deck and observed, trying hard to hide their desperation.

Brody did not bother to step on board. He offered Charlie his hand and said, "I appreciate your taking the time. It would have been nice to do business with my old place. But we'll be heading for Radio Island. You understand."

"Hang on, hang on." Charlie slumped, offering a theatrical gesture for the sake of the watchful owners. "There's no need to head out. We've got plenty—"

"You heard the lady," Brody warned. "We're on the clock here."

Charlie followed them back down the pier. "What exactly does that mean?"

"I want to lease the boat now. If it passes an ocean trial," he paused for emphasis, then added, "cash buy."

Charlie studied the two of them a moment longer, then pointed to the marina's furthest pier. "I might have just the thing."

As soon as the vessel came into view, Brody announced, "This is perfect."

Out of the corner of his eye he spotted Rae frowning, and knew she thought it was a foul way to start negotiations. But they didn't have time for dickering.

"There's nothing official," Charlie said, cagey now. "But for the right price . . . what?"

Charlie stopped because Brody had offered the marina chief his hand a second time. "It's a great boat, Charlie. And I appreciate you showing us what you have here. It clarifies what to aim for. But like the lady said, we don't have time for any dance."

Charlie backed away from Brody's hand. "Now you just wait a second!"

But Brody was already starting toward the truck. "Come on, Rae. Let's go see what they have at the Radio Island Marina. It's larger, and they usually stock a few new—"

"I said wait, now. Just gimme long enough to make a call."

"No call. Not yet." Brody gave him stone. "Let's make sure we're clear on terms. First, I lease the boat. I'm asking for three days, but I'll settle for two. Give it an ocean trial. At the end of this time, the owner gives me a price. Straight from the horse's mouth. Owner to buyer. I mean what I say, Charlie. It's an up or down deal. I don't dicker."

Charlie's inspection was tight now, almost approving. "I know they're not coming down for the holidays because they told me. What if I could get you a lease through New Year's Day?"

"Better still, long as the lease price goes toward the final purchase."

He offered Brody a tight nod. "Let me see if I can reach them. Might as well let me run your card." As he started away, he added, "Get a load of this. Little Brody Reames. All grown up."

Soon as Charlie came back and confirmed the deal was moving forward, the marina chief became almost chatty. He described the owners as his-and-hers hyperachievers. They held down high-powered jobs in the Research Triangle Park west of Raleigh. To celebrate the birth of their first child, they bought this boat and started making plans for early retirement so they could up stakes and sail around the world.

But their daughter hated the open water. Charlie described a four-year-old who had to be dragged kicking and screaming from the car. How she wept and begged not to be taken on board.

When they took overnight sails, just the two of them, a weekend proved more than enough time away from their little girl. Then child number two came along, then dual promotions, and this past summer the boat never left the marina. Charlie did the necessary engine maintenance, cleaned below the waterline, scrubbed the bilges, and was ready when the couple said it was too much boat to leave tied up dockside. The engine had less than eighty hours run time, the electronics were state of the art. On and on Charlie went, clearly loving the boat.

While Charlie nattered, Brody gave the craft a thorough check, from bow to sails to bilges. All the while, Rae sat on the skipper's chair, occasionally running her hand around the ship's helm. The stainless steel wheel measured a full five feet across. When Charlie left to deal with another client, Rae asked, "Why do you like this boat so much?"

Brody leaned against the port gunnel and stared through the open hatch leading into the main cabin. "Some say the J Boat is the world's best combination of racing craft and family cruisers."

She shook the wheel, back and forth like a happy child. "Tell me why."

"The J Class racing yachts originated in 1903. They were founded on what's now known as the Universal Rule, a calculation of sail and keel and boat's measurements. It was invented by Nathaniel Herreshoff as a way to maximize speed and stability. It's a brilliant concept, Rae. A mathematically precise method of balancing . . . what?"

"I wish you could see yourself. Go on. Tell me more about old Nat's rule."

"You're making fun."

"I don't care about the math, Brody. Talk to me about the boat."

"The J/112e is a modern rendition of this same mathematical construct. It's won every build award in the world. And for good reason. A boat this size can easily be handled by one sailor."

Her hand froze. "That's what you want, to head into the sunset like some lone water-bound cowboy?"

The solemn way she watched him now, the intense manner, pushed his heart into overdrive. Time slowed to where he could take careful note of the tiniest elements. A single moment captured by a lovely woman's question. Not what she asked, but what she meant.

Brody tasted the tangy mix of seaweed and winter wind and marina, a flavor he had loved his entire life. It felt so good to speak of such things here. "Rae, I've never dreamed I might someday have a lady to share this with."

It was her turn to go quiet. They might have stayed like that for hours. Days, even. Except Brody heard Charlie's footsteps hurrying back down the pier. As they turned to greet him, he heard Rae murmur, "And that's the right answer."

15

They stopped for sandwiches at the Beaufort Café. Diners at the lone outdoor table departed as they emerged from his truck, so Rae claimed it while Brody went inside and ordered. The wind whispered a chilly promise when he emerged, speaking of the day to come. He set down their plates, went back for their drinks, then said, "I'm having trouble processing what's just happened."

"Let me see if I have this straight," Rae said, then paused for a bite. She swallowed, sipped her tea, then said, "You're fretting over the idea of buying the most beautiful boat you've ever laid eyes on."

He resisted the urge to reach across and wipe the mayonnaise from her lip. "Something like that."

"I know, it's a terrible thing." Another bite. More tea. "Not to mention how you might spend tomorrow sailing with a couple of lifetime pals."

"You are that, aren't you," Brody replied, his heart suddenly overfull. "My lifetime friend."

She gave him the sort of look only a woman could accomplish, inviting him to just dive straight in.

That is, if he was actually reading this right.

But all she said was, "You're worried about the cost?"

"I haven't gotten that far. But yeah. I'll definitely need a loan, if they even offer that for a boat. I've saved pretty much everything I've made, and I can sell my condo, pay off the mortgage, and see what's left."

The finger she raised glistened with mayo. "I've been thinking about that. What if we agreed to the lord viscount's conditions, with one caveat. You're giving up two years' bonus to accept his offer."

"Jacob hasn't agreed—"

"Don't interrupt an attorney. All the hot air could build up and explode, and you'd be cleaning up a real mess."

"Go on, then."

"We request a signing bonus. Then we ask for the lord high muckety-muck's company to grant you an interest-free loan for the balance."

Brody stared across the tiny iron table. "Okay, this is me, totally freaked."

"You like?"

"Rae, I like everything about you." He jerked back a fraction. "Sorry. Totally out of line."

That particular comment silenced the table. They finished their meal, gathered the plates and cups, returned to the truck, started away. Not a word. Nada.

Emma proved well enough to have dressed herself, and now made it down the front stairs on her own steam. Brody watched as she took tiny careful steps, both hands gripping the banister with white-knuckle intensity. But still.

Once they were settled and underway, Brody asked, "I'd like to call my sister and let her know we're coming."

"I don't want people making a fuss." But Emma was smiling.

She rode in front with Rae seated directly behind her. Rae had one hand draped over Emma's shoulder, and as Brody called his sister Emma reached up and touched Rae's hand.

Olivia's voice came through the truck's speakers. "What have you done now?"

"I thought you'd like to know I'm driving Emma to the hospital."

"Why, what's the matter?"

"Nothing," Emma replied. "I just don't want Doctor Nasty in my bedroom ever again."

"I guess that works. Hi, Emma."

"Hello, dear."

"We were about to head down to a Christmas party. Want some supermarket cake made with pure white sugar and lard and icing out of a box?"

"Just what I dreamed about when I got up this morning," Rae offered.

Brody stopped at a light, glanced over, and saw the two women smiling. He told his sister, "I'll stop by soon as the patient is settled."

"Don't you dare call me that ever again," Emma said, still smiling.

Olivia said, "Whack the boy once for me, Emma."

When they pulled into the visitor's lot, Cameron emerged through the hospital's side door with Olivia. Both were dressed in red felt hats adorned with tiny antlers. Emma waited until she was settled into the wheelchair to offer, "Shame on you, leaving those poor patients to fret and suffer while you're out here playing like nine-year-olds."

"Nobody got sick today," Olivia replied, leaning over and giving Emma a gentle hug. "Whole hospital's empty."

Cameron took her place and said, "The nurses and surgeons are turning the surgical ward into a bingo hall."

Brody was about to volunteer putting a disco ball in the cafeteria when his mother stepped through the door. "Mom?"

"Surprise." She smiled a greeting at Rae, then bent

over and held Emma for the longest time. "How are you, dear?"

"Coping. Most days, anyway. And you?"

Olivia said, "She was in town ordering furniture for the two studios. I invited her over for cake."

"I would not touch that supermarket poison wearing gloves and a gown," Mia replied. To Emma, "I'm doing well enough, considering." She reached for Brody. "Hello, son."

Emma announced, "Brody is taking one of my cabins for the duration."

"He told me. Given the circumstances, I think that's wise. Now why don't we all get out of the cold."

They filled the elevator and paraded along the upstairs corridor, where a receptionist personally took control of Emma's chair. Brody held to the rear position as the receptionist knocked on a closed door, and at a word from inside, she opened it and wheeled Emma inside.

The young, sharp-featured doctor continued to type into his computer, ignoring Emma and the others. Then he looked up and saw Brody's mother standing in the open doorway. He rose from his chair. "Mrs. Reames. Good afternoon."

"Hello, Kendrick. I hope your parents are both doing well."

"Yes, ma'am."

"Please remember me to them." Mia stepped to one side, allowing the receptionist to depart. "Emma is one of my very dearest friends. It's so good to know her needs are being seen to by such a capable doctor."

The doctor took in all the faces crowded into his doorway behind Mia. "Certainly."

"I can't tell you how much it means, knowing you will take special care of this sweet and wonderful woman." The internist was still standing as Mia gently shut the door.

They walked straight past the cafeteria, which had been transformed into a boisterous and happy place, full of hospital staff and ambulatory patients and families and music and Christmas cheer. Olivia led them up one flight and along a confusing series of halls. She stopped midway down a stubby corridor and did a little "ta-dah." A wall of glass stretched out in both directions. Behind it, masked technicians in protective gear worked at lab tables filled with equipment. Several of them stopped and offered happy waves, then resumed work. Olivia gave a superswift rundown of their ongoing analyses, then offered to check everyone's blood and bone marrow and spinal fluid, free of charge, Christmas special. That made for a superswift, laughing departure.

Another confusing series of corridors later, they entered Cameron's office. She snagged a plate of cookies off her receptionist's desk, took orders for drinks, asked her aide to phone downstairs and check on Emma's progress, then led them inside. The receptionist entered with a tray of coffees, reported that Emma was booked in for another scan but should be done within the hour.

Cameron's private office was surprisingly spacious. Brody settled on the sofa opposite the windows. The four women—Rae and Cameron and Olivia and Mia—gathered by a small cherrywood table holding three hardback chairs. Cameron drew over her office chair and pointed to a fourth chair by the side wall, inviting him to join them. Brody smiled and thanked her and remained where he was. He liked observing them as they chatted, not keeping him out so much as joining together in the easy manner of old friends. He was happy remaining a welcome visitor to this moment.

Sharp winter sunlight pushed through Cameron's gauzy drapes, casting the room and occupants in brilliant pastels. Brody sipped his coffee and wondered at how comfortable he felt while seated here in the therapist's office. As long as he remained in the Outer Banks, this would become a place for revealing secrets, elements that had shaped him. Stripping away the barriers he had spent a lifetime building. And which now he was intent on casting aside. Making room for—what, exactly? In this moment, Brody realized he really didn't care. He hoped his current state was not merely the aftereffect of this incredible morning. Emma better, more time with Rae, the heady prospect of a new job, a wonderful boat that might someday become his. He had every reason to feel jazzed.

Yet Brody sensed something more was at work. A deeper sentiment running like an unseen ocean current, while all he saw were the surface effects.

It was weird, being so happy in a place designed to pry open secret doors and reveal hidden mysteries. Brody corrected himself. Happiness suggested a temporary high, at least for him. His current state suggested something else. He was happy, yes, but he was also content.

Mia chose that moment to disengage from the group and walk back to his corner. "Scootch over, son." When she was settled, she said, "This is so like how I remember you. Finding a quiet haven, observing the world."

"With Dad around, it was my safest option." He waited, expecting a rebuke. When his mother merely settled further into the sofa, Brody knew it was time.

He swiveled slightly, facing her. "Dad is going to come after you. His arrogance won't allow you to walk away. His need to dominate is too great."

Mia sat calmly, hands in her lap, watching her

daughter chatter with the other two ladies. Brody caught something about Cameron's upcoming baby shower. It was like overhearing a conversation from a distant room.

Brody was astonished that Mia had let him get this far. His mother had a lifetime's experience at deflecting any such complaint.

Today was definitely one for the books.

He went on, "I know what Dad is planning. It came to me full-blown last night. Do you want—?"

"No." Quiet. Firm. Definite. "No."

"I won't let him do this to you. Please don't ask me to back away. He can't be allowed to damage us like this. I won't let it."

Mia remained silent. Unmoving. Watching her daughter.

Olvia must have noticed the strain he was feeling, for she looked over and asked, "Everything all right?"

"Give us a moment, dear." Mia waited until the three ladies resumed their conversation to say, "Go on, son."

"I had planned to work through Rae. She's my attorney now, we're involved in another negotiation . . ." He waved that aside. Later. "I know now I need to handle this myself." Speaking the words aloud left him so nauseous, he pressed a fist deep into his gut, fighting down the gorge. He finished, "Face-to-face."

"It will destroy your relationship."

"Mom, has there ever been anything to destroy? I mean, really?"

Mia took her time, observing the ladies, handling the moment as she had so much else. Then: "When will this happen?"

"I think . . . tomorrow." He pressed his fist deeper still. "We're taking Emma sailing. I'd like to do this first."

"Then go out into the open water and cleanse it all away." She nodded. "When are you moving into Emma's cottage?"

"Later today."

"Good. I'm glad you'll be close at hand. In case you're needed."

And suddenly the strain was gone. Swept away so completely, he might as well never have felt the immensity of confronting his old man. Brody unclenched his fist. Leaned back. Took a deep breath. Looked at Cameron, the woman helping to unlock those hidden portals.

He was no longer the frightened child.

Mia rose and stood looking down at him. "You understood I'm not allowing this to happen on my behalf."

Brody did not respond.

Mia smiled approval at his silence. She gestured

him to rise, and embraced him. "It's so good to see you coming into your own."

Brody stood there, watching his mother rejoin the others, four women melded together by the pastel light. And reached a new decision.

He would do it today.

16

Brody said nothing the entire journey back to Emma's. He kept waiting for the fear to strike, the tension that gripped him whenever he met his father. Instead, he felt nothing at all. The journey was pleasant enough, Emma smiling as Rae chatted about tomorrow. Occasionally, Rae said something about the lovely boat, expecting him to chime in. But the boat and the coming sea voyage belonged to a different realm. He drove, and he smiled and nodded in the right places, but he was already set on a different course. Even so, the usual storm of emotions did not arrive.

Emma was definitely worn out from the day. Brody more or less carried her up the stairs and through the bookstore. The neighbor on volunteer duty was a heavyset woman whose multiple bracelets clinked nervously as she lifted one hand to her mouth and said, "Emma, what on earth?"

"Do us all a favor, dear," Emma replied. "And give me a break."

Brody couldn't help chuckling.

Emma glared at him. "In case you were wondering, young man, I can also do without your attitude."

Same old Emma.

Rae helped her settle into bed, multiple pillows propping her into a seated position. Emma thanked them, then declared, "I think this calls for Chinese."

Rae replied, "Yum."

"Mongolian beef. Kung pow chicken."

"Veggies," Rae said.

"Every plate needs a little garnish," Emma agreed. When Rae turned towards him, she added, "Brody is otherwise occupied. Aren't you, dear."

He had actually been thinking how grabbing Chinese to go and dining with the ladies was a perfect excuse to delay things. "I could do this for you."

"No, dear. You can't."

Her response took Brody straight back. Emma had the same ability as his mother, to chide and sympathize and direct with a smile.

Rae demanded, "What is going on here?"

Emma held Brody with her gaze. "Did you bring your things with you?"

"In the truck."

"Grab the key to number six on your way out. You can move in when you're done."

Brody wondered if his mother had said something when he wasn't looking. Or if Emma had found a way to pierce time's veil. He merely bent over, kissed her cheek, and headed out. As he started down the corridor, he heard Rae say, "As the attorney of record, I demand to know what you two are not telling me."

Brody headed east on 70, waiting for the panic to strike. He had driven this highway so often, he could list all the landmarks by rote. Especially the industrial park containing his father's company.

The turnoff had been reduced to near gravel by all the heavy traffic. Two farm equipment companies with their supply and repair depots flanked the juncture. A road contractor came next, with their gravel yard and chemicals warehouses across the street. And finally, there at the back, a hurricane fence surrounded Reames Construction.

Brody cut the motor and rose from the car and started toward the main office. The single-story building was simple and functional, rimmed by a patch of miniature trees and flowering shrubs, mostly winter brown. His mother's work. From the warehouse to his right, Brody heard loud voices. They weren't angry, and they weren't shouting. These were people who built and dug and worked hard. They were in the habit of talking loud enough to be heard over construction equipment. Brody had been around such people all his life. Some he really liked. When he started working for his uncle, they welcomed him—some who worked for his father, others he got to know at the boatyard. He had become one of them, even at that young age. They all knew his father, and they made allowances. Any number of those men and women had come from similar backgrounds. Or worse. They didn't talk about it, because there was nothing to say.

As Brody approached the offices he heard his father's bark. That single sharp note was enough to silence the yard. Brody kept waiting for the tension, the dread that had defined his earlier years.

Nothing.

Whenever he thought of his father, the memories held a sense of impossible burdens. Of never measuring up. Today he was simply carrying out a necessary act. He climbed the front steps and opened the door and stepped inside. Not even his own accelerated heart rate could touch him.

Janet sat precisely where she'd always been. A three-pack-a-day smoker who adored Brody's dad and loved how he didn't seem to care or even notice that she always had a cigarette going. Brody's entrance caught her in the act of lighting up. The flame froze inches from her cigarette. She clicked off the lighter and said, "Look what we got here. The handsome pirate back from the sea." Janet reached out. "Come give an old lady a hug."

It was like embracing an ash tray. Brody always greeted her the same way. "I'm amazed Health and Safety hasn't locked you up."

"They can't find me in all the smoke." She flicked the lighter, then pointed at the side window. "Your pop's out there somewhere riling the troops."

He headed back. "I'm just picking up some things for Mom."

"Hang on there, handsome."

It was only when Brody turned around that he realized the office held no Christmas ornaments whatsoever.

Janet demanded, "Are you sure that's wise?"

Brody decided there was nothing more to be said. As he started down the hall, he was momentarily halted by the wooden panel bolted to the wall above his father's office door. Burned into the varnished slab were the same words that greeted every visitor to their home: MY ROOF, MY RULES.

Janet called, "Brody?"

"I won't be long."

* * *

His mother's former office was incredibly neat. He had visited any number of times. It did not appear as though anything had been shifted, which was what Brody had been counting on. Mia's departure had shocked the company as much as his father. They all probably expected Emmett Reames to wait until the new year before seeking a replacement. The flower vase on her side credenza was empty, and it appeared that someone had dusted. But otherwise, the place was exactly the same. Even the family photos were still on the wall.

Brody knew exactly what needed doing. He started up the computer and keyed in the same password Mia used on every device—the numerical birth dates of her children in order of arrival.

Then he realized he had forgotten to bring a memory stick.

The desk was locked. But the top drawer had been broken for years. Brody gripped it with both hands and pressed and lifted. The drawer came free. He searched with nervous hands and found the internal catch, releasing all the others. To his vast relief, the middle right drawer held a trio of USB drives still in their packaging. His anxious fingers fumbled as he unwrapped and slid one home.

Brody had no idea what precise form his father's attack would take. So he downloaded everything. All the files, purchases to contracts to revenue to taxes. He was fairly certain the poison would be inserted in something from the past six to twelve months. The further back any alteration went, the more complicated a web they would need to spin. But just to be certain, he added all the files going back three years. If nothing else, it would help them show a clear pattern of honest dealing. The trademarks that defined Mia Reames.

He heard a chair scrape somewhere, followed by a heavy tread. The front door opened and closed. Brody figured Janet had gone to fetch his father.

The racing heart, the nervous hands. The eerie calm. So very similar to all those earlier episodes. And yet entirely different. Utterly new.

The front door slammed back and his father's work boots scraped across the foyer. The sound evoked a blister of memories. How Brody always shot to his feet at the sound of Emmett Reames on approach. Today he merely breathed around the torrent of memories and emotions. Not safe. Never here. Even so, he maintained that same distance. The calm, the fear, the nerves, the drumming heart. Brody heard

Janet's murmur following along behind as Emmett Reames marched down the main corridor. Brody checked the download status, strangely glad he had left Mia's door open. There was no barrier here, no masking his intent.

Emmett Reames entered so swiftly he pushed a cloud of cigarette smoke in with him. Which, under different circumstances, might have made for a moment's bitter humor.

Brody heard his father panting.

The sound was beyond strange, almost unique. Emmett Reames took immense pride in controlling himself as well as his surroundings. He was a small man, not quite touching five-nine, very compact, and radiating a constant tension. Brush-cut steel-gray hair, boxer's jaw, hunter's tight glacial gaze. Brody had often heard Emmett Reames described as Carolina's very own Napoleon, a moniker his father took pride in. He wore his standard weekday outfit of carefully ironed denims, his pale blue shirt so starched it remained creased even after he had sweat it dark. His standard nod to winter was a fleece vest.

"I should have known they'd send you," he told Brody. "Since you've spent a lifetime hiding behind women's skirts."

Hearing those words emerging from a second man that day was good for a bitter smile.

"You think I'm funny?" Emmett's tone became razor sharp. "Stand up when I'm talking to you!"

Brody remained where he was. "I spent my entire life thinking I was the problem."

Emmett snorted. "At least you got that much right."

"That and wishing I could be the son you wanted."

"You'll never be. Not in a million years. Now tell me what you're doing in my business."

But he wasn't finished. "I know now that wasn't the issue. It never has been. The real issue, then and now, is you're incapable of accepting who I am."

"Why should I? My roof, my rules! You were too dumb to ever get that through your thick head!" The computer chimed. Emmett watched Brody pull the drive from the USB slot and rise to his feet. "Give me that!"

"No."

Emmett started across the office, rage boiling.

"What are you going to do, Pop? Assault your son in front of witnesses?"

He hesitated. Another first. Glanced back at wide-eyed Janet in the doorway. Snarled, "That's grand larceny."

"Surprising way to describe making a record of your bookkeeper's work." Brody rounded the desk and moved into his father's space. "Keeping things safe. And honest. And out in the open. The way Mom always worked. Isn't that right?"

He was close enough for Brody to smell the mint on his breath. "I'll grind you into dust."

"You've been trying to do that my entire life." Brody stepped past Janet and started down the corridor. "Look how far that's gotten you."

17

Rae went for Chinese, dined with Emma in her bedroom, then departed after Emma swatted the air irritatingly and ordered her out. Every minute with this exasperating, cantankerous woman was a gift. Every second. Rae headed for her office, determined to dive into the pile of administrivia she'd been putting off. Spend the rest of the afternoon immersed in legalese.

Amiya phoned just as Rae crossed the Radio Island bridge. "Emma told me about your sailing adventure. I am hoping to bribe my way on board. If there's room."

"Room is not an issue. Brody has found us an amazing boat."

"Is that a yes, I can come?"

"I'm an attorney. I am open to negotiations."

"You also happen to be *my* attorney."

"Sorry. Conflict of interest and all that."

"I have no idea what you just said."

"We were discussing bribes."

"Two loaves of still warm sourdough. All kinds of cheese. Grapes and pears and such. Emma has requested wine. I suppose I could spring for that as well."

Rae confessed, "I forgot all about food."

"When I told Emma what I had in mind, she said it's to be her best Christmas feast ever. That has to count for something, even with an attorney who's trying to make things difficult."

They were still making plans when her phone chimed with another incoming call.

Holden.

Rae apologized with words she did not actually hear, cut the connection, accepted the new call, and said, "Holden, hi."

His voice was not battleground crisp, but close. "Where are you, Rae?"

"Just leaving Morehead for the island. What—"

"Can we meet at your office?"

There was no reason this conversation should send her heart into overdrive. None whatsoever. "Five minutes."

Rae parked behind her little apartment and walked the two blocks to her office. A chilly ocean breeze swirled about the stubby island buildings, pushing and twisting and seeking somewhere to pounce. The streets and sidewalks were empty. Rae felt the wind work through her clothes, nibble at her neck and hands and ankles, then she turned the corner and forgot about the cold, the day, Emma, everything.

Standing there in front of her office door was Holden.

As she approached, the wind took on a new purpose. It reached into her mind and, with cold and clinical precision, began unraveling her tangled thoughts. They formed two distinct lines. One to be shared with Holden. The other strictly for her.

The divided mental process held a distinct clarity. The secret portion of this dialogue focused on just one thought: This fine man deserved better than she had offered.

Holden said in greeting, "I don't like the way you talked to me."

She so enjoyed looking at this man. The balanced features, the clear-eyed calm, his gentle manner, the hidden power, the mystery, the secret blade.

"Twice," Holden said. "I didn't like it at all."

Rae's words became fashioned from the biting wind. "You deserve better," she replied. "Kindness, warmth." She started to add an additional word. *Love.* But cut that off and left it unspoken.

"Not your courtroom voice," Holden agreed.

"I hurt you, speaking the way I did," Rae acknowledged.

"A lot," he agreed.

"I'm sorry." The dual strands were fully separated now. She saw him with a lover's heart and an attorney's brain. "You're a very good man. I should have started with that. And ended with it as well."

"Why didn't you?"

"Those two moments you chose to talk about feelings. And a future. Us. Together. It was the worst possible timing."

"Why didn't you tell me that?"

"I tried to, remember?" When he remained silent, she continued, "I had no bandwidth to respond emotionally. I offered you what I had."

"I feel like I'm getting more of the same now."

That surprised her, for internally she felt as if her emotions were there in every word. It felt as if the wind sighed for her. "Emma is not well. I told you that. I feel like everything else inside my world has been put on hold. Especially my emotions."

"That's tough," Holden allowed. "I know how much she means to you."

Actually, he didn't. This from the attorney. And suddenly the silent conversation came to dominate, forming a string of questions. Most were those she asked herself at the close of every romantic chapter. Was this her lifelong fate? Did she force her men away because of some unknown flaw? Did she select men she knew were not lifelong material? And so forth.

Her heart responded as it often did in her predawn chats. Weeping internal tears, wishing and aching for what she did not have. Fearing it might never be hers to claim. And yet . . .

Sprinkled among these old painful questions were a few she had not faced before.

Was she ready, finally, at long last, to give herself fully? Was a lifelong commitment truly where she had arrived?

Was it Holden?

Had it ever been?

And with that, her heart went silent.

Rae asked, "Why are you here? I'm sorry, that came out totally wrong. I meant, why are you here now?"

"I'm going away."

"On a job?"

He might have nodded, but if so, it was barely a fractional shift. Like he had motioned against his will. Or better judgment. Something.

Rae added, "And you can't or don't want to talk about it."

"Confidentiality is a vital part of our service," Holden replied. Now he was the one showing her a clinical tone. "Revealing our task or destination is cause for instant dismissal. This defines our work and sets us apart."

Rae added the last part for him. "You don't think I should have demanded to be let in."

"I spoke to you about intimacy and a shared tomorrow. You played the lawyer."

"That's what I am, Holden. An attorney at law. It defines and shapes my life. For us to be together permanently, we need a union that includes this. Really. Otherwise, our lives can never be forged as one."

He was ready for that. "Most couples do fine, keeping work separate."

"That isn't how I want to live."

She actually saw the door close in his gaze. Holden on one side, she on the other. He opened his mouth to respond, then just turned and walked away.

Rae stood and watched until he was swallowed by the afternoon light. She did not feel regret so much as old. Entering her office and crossing the front room formed a legendary trek. She settled into her office chair and just sat there, too aged and ancient to do more than breathe.

Finally, she did the only thing that came to mind.

Regardless of how utterly illogical it was. Rae Alden, the attorney, withered down to where she acted on instinct alone. She texted Brody. A solitary cry for help. Just two words. All she could manage.

Call me.

18

After leaving his father's, Brody stopped for Mexican. He was not particularly hungry, but he wanted to put a space between the confrontation and everything that came next. The taqueria was a favorite with his former crew, and he ran a risk coming here. But he loved the food, and he arrived between the lunchtime work crowd and the dinner crunch. A few families were eating, the children chatting musically, the parents quiet and tired and smiling.

He took his order to an empty table and ate slowly. Every now and then a bolt of memory struck. Single flashes of an image that came and went in seconds. Afterward, his body hummed, a temporary shift away from his placid state. A glimpse of his father's rage. The acidic strike of words that could not stab as they always had before. The sight of Janet's fearful gaze. Smoke boiling into his mother's office. On the surface, it had been merely another minor confrontation.

A few words spoken in bitter wrath, just another father–son drama. Only this time the power to wrench his life from its course and fracture his days was absent. Brody found his attention increasingly pulled away from the argument to his own calmness.

He finished eating, thanked the staff, and deflected their question over why he hadn't come earlier with the rest of Jacob's crew. Not even that could touch him. As he rejoined Highway 70 and headed toward the Beaufort bridges, Brody's peace was threatened by the fear that life had made a mistake. That he didn't deserve this amazing day, a chance to truly break free. That sooner or later, the world would wake up to who he had been and was fated to remain, and would strip away this incredible moment.

Then he climbed the Radio Island bridge, and the waters sparkled and beckoned, laced as they were with the rising wind. His peace returned. At least for this one moment. It was enough. And far more than he deserved.

Brody pulled in behind Emma's home and parked by Cottage Six. The afternoon light formed blades through the trio of trees forming the lawn's central island. As he climbed from the truck, the empty garden became filled with ghosts.

In the weeks running up to leaving Charlotte, these sudden appearances had become part of his nights. Faces of scarcely remembered ladies floated into his vision, silently condemning him to a cage of guilt and remorse.

Today, however, was different.

There, among those he had cast aside and forgotten, were others.

Friends and family he no longer determinedly kept out. Women who were coming to trust him. Despite everything. These were the ones who accompanied him up the cottage's front steps.

As he crossed the front porch, Brody felt as if the calm now had both a purpose and a name. Facing up to his past was helping him make space for a different future. What shape that might take, he had no idea. But one thing was for certain. The days ahead now possessed an element of hope.

He dropped his gear on the bare kitchen table and took a quick look around. He had been in and out of these guesthouses for years, doing odd jobs, being helpful, trying to show Emma how much she had always meant. The interior was no great shakes, but lovely just the same. Two smallish bedrooms, a single bath, the spacious front room. The heating had been off long enough for the floor and walls to radiate a distinct chill. Brody worked the controls, then returned to the front porch and stood there, growing accustomed to this new space in his world. The calm was there waiting for him, a weightless sensation.

Brody felt it all come together. Wind and sea and light and dark.

He turned on his phone. There were eleven texts, three from his mother, seven from his sister. Which meant his mother had told Olivia what was happening. The most recent, though, was from Rae, and held just two words. Call me.

He touched the callback, mostly because he needed to say the words pushing up from his chest. A declaration that needed to be released. Now. While it still burned his heart and throat.

Soon as she came on the line, Brody said, "I know I'm not the only man who has a lady's tears staining his past. Right now, though, I'm the one trying to make amends."

Rae rewarded him with silence.

Brody went on, "I've lived my life like a kid with nothing to lose. It's time I grow up and take responsibility for my actions. Learn what it means to give myself fully to the moment, and to the people I care for and who care for me. Accept the challenge of far horizons."

He stopped then. Wishing for better words. Rae deserved them, whatever they might be.

Rae knew what she was going to do long before Brody finished describing the confrontation with his father. All the residue from her conversation with Holden was gone. Smoke in the wind. Less.

Brody needed what she could offer. His attorney. And his friend. Everything else could definitely wait until her heart's bruises had eased.

Brody's sister had mentioned Harvey Sewell was the attorney representing their father in the divorce. She asked Brody to wait one second, long enough to switch over and text him. She asked Harvey for ten minutes of his time, less, regarding an urgent legal matter, and she was coming over now. Then she was back on the call with Brody, telling him to continue, slinging her purse and locking up, and heading for her car. She scurried the two blocks, not quite running, totally immune to the wind and the cold. She started the engine and put Brody on hands-free. Then she sat there, listening to the man and her own internal voice. When she spoke again, it was to ask, "How do you feel?" A question directed as much to herself as Brody.

She listened to Brody describe doing his best to clear away the detritus of past mistakes. Making room for a future he could not name. The man sounded shaken, sorrowful. Yet calm. A remarkable mixture of smoke and honey.

When he finished speaking, Rae thanked him for sharing. Brody asked, "Is there anything in particular we need to discuss? Your text sounded urgent to me."

"It was. Very." She started to tell him where she was headed, then decided that could definitely wait. "I needed to hear from a friend."

Brody breathed on that for a time, then replied, "I like having you consider me that, Rae. A friend."

"I do."

"I like that a lot." Another breath. "Can I come see you?"

"There's the small matter of me being an attorney, with attorney-type things that need doing."

"Oh. That."

"Yeah. That."

"So what time are we hitting the water tomorrow?"

"Emma's been sleeping in lately. By the time she's up and breakfasted and ready, my guess is late morning."

"In that case I'll head over to the marina around eight, check in with Charlie, then ready the boat. Make coffee, sit behind the wheel, pretend I belong."

Rae cut the connection and sat at the final light before taking the island bridge. Thinking about Brody's first words, how precisely they fit into her heart's vacant space. The right thing to say at the perfect moment.

She felt as if the door to her inner world was flung wide open. Despite the terrible timing, Emma's declining health, all the pressures and uncertainties that filled her days. She had so very much that she wanted to say. To Brody. About feelings. And tomorrows. And them. Together.

The biggest change, at least for her, was how her perspective on Holden had altered. She no longer saw their latest conversation as yet another failure. Instead, Rae now felt as if she too was making room for something more.

All her logic and careful strategies were cast aside. She wanted to be with Brody Reames. She wanted . . .

The huge expanse of that unfinished declaration filled in her mind and body until there wasn't room to draw a decent breath.

19

Harvey Sewell had recently moved into a new waterfront home. A dozen or so similar minimansions extended along the river northeast of Beaufort. Locals called the neighborhood Little Miami and scorned the wealthy owners who only resided there a few weeks each high season. These same people formed a sizable portion of Harvey's clientele. Earlier that autumn, Harvey had closed his Morehead office and shifted to the home's ground floor. Rae had of course never visited, but she had heard the new digs perfectly suited Harvey's overblown ego.

Rae parked in the circular drive and entered by way of glass-paneled double doors. The downstairs antechamber held a chandelier, a sweeping staircase, a granite and onyx floor, an elevator, and doors to a lovely conference room. Harvey's outer office was empty, but the doors to his inner sanctum were open.

He waved her in, pointed to the phone planted to his ear, and raised a single finger.

Rae did a slow circle, taking in Harvey's three hand-blown chandeliers, two Persian carpets, and a desk nearly as big as Brody's boat. She took up position by the rear window and resumed the internal dialogue she had started on the way over. It had very little to do with Holden, which she found very interesting. Holden was, quite simply, absent. Nor was she all that concerned about the coming conversation with Harvey. Again, interesting. Normally she spent hours prepping, going over her lines like an actor preparing for the stage. Not today.

Instead, Rae dissected her own feelings about her future.

What was wrong with wanting a true lifetime partnership? Why couldn't she seek a love that was big enough and sufficiently grand to include profession, job, work, hopes, aims? Because that's what she wanted. A three-course lifelong feast. Like the contract stated. For better or worse.

"Rae Alden, as I live and breathe!" Harvey stepped around his desk with hand outstretched. His smile was as polished as his nails. Even on an office-casual day he wore a striped shirt with cufflinks glittering in the afternoon light. Carolina Panther suspenders accented the bulge of his substantial gut. "Please tell me you're not collecting for another charity."

"Not today."

"In that case, welcome to my humble abode!" He made a process of ushering her over and holding the chair as she settled. "I swear, there's been such a parade of folks with their hands out. I was ready to lock up and hibernate."

"Thank you so much for seeing me." Harvey's office took full use of the view, with a wall of floor-to-ceiling glass sliders framed by drapes matching his carpets. The full expanse of islands and water and horizon was partially blocked, however, by a massive yacht. "You certainly have a lovely home."

"Kind of you to say." He settled into his executive chair and swept a hand over the documents piled on his desk. "Sorry I can't show you upstairs. But there's work I have to complete before year's end."

"Of course." Normally Rae entered such confrontations with her moves carefully mapped out in advance. This time, such preparations were impossible. She only had Brody's word to go on. Rae was fairly certain his view of the situation was correct. It fit perfectly with everything she knew about this attorney and his tactics.

Just the same, she had to be certain.

Rae started, "I understand you represent Mr. Emmett Reames in the ongoing divorce proceedings."

"That is correct." He pretended to search the files

on his desk. "I'm sorry, I don't recall seeing your name mentioned."

"This is a recent development."

Harvey extracted a file, but left it unopened. "No one informed me of a change in legal representation."

"I represent the children in this matter. When is the court date?"

"January seventh." His bonhomie was gone now. "The Reames children have an attorney?"

"One does. The son. This will perhaps soon change to include the daughter as well."

Harvey only hesitated an instant. But those few seconds were all the confirmation Rae needed. He said, "Adult children bringing their own legal representation to their parents' divorce is hardly necessary." His hand tapped the closed file. "Or even what might be considered standard legal procedure."

Rae should not have been enjoying herself so much. Real futures of real lives were at stake here. Just the same, she could have bounced in her seat like a child on a trampoline. Harvey was already unsettled, and she hadn't even gotten to the juicy bits. Which was hardly a surprise, given their history. "But in certain cases, such representation is vital. And the court has agreed on numerous occasions."

Harvey's desk was absurdly large. He might as well offer visitors binoculars and a megaphone. "I suppose in such a case having an observer might be useful."

Rae dropped the hand that had halted him in midflow. "I would not be present as an observer."

"But . . . This is a divorce."

"If financial impropriety is involved, the children's legal representative can be added to the proceedings."

"Nonsense."

"Again, there are numerous precedents."

"Ridiculous."

"Dozens of them. Local, state, federal. Right up the food chain."

"Well, be that as it may . . . *What?*"

"How many times have you faced me in court, Harvey?"

Silence.

"Five. Five times. And in each and every case, I have, to put it in strict legalese, handed you your hat." It was her turn to offer an insincere smile. "As you are no doubt aware, financial discovery can be made part of any divorce proceeding."

Harvey's bluster was a well-known component of his courtroom antics. "You have no idea what you're involving yourself in here."

"Actually, I do. Since my client has for years been involved in finance. We are in possession of corporate financial records, tax and otherwise, going back years.

My client is concerned that the court will be presented with so-called secondary corporate accounts, supposedly revealing how funds have been siphoned off."

Harvey might as well have stopped breathing.

His silence was all the confirmation Rae required. "If that is the case, you and your client might suggest to the court this has only been discovered since the company's bookkeeper resigned. And perhaps also suggest your client has suspected for years that his firm should have been more profitable than it was. And now you have evidence of theft. Or at least, you might so claim to the court."

As she spoke, Harvey's features grew a sheen of perspiration. "You only think you know what's going on."

"You will present your evidence, and I will present mine. The court will decide who is telling the truth." She rose from the chair. Smiling, gentle voiced, all sweetness and light. "As an officer of the court, you are no doubt aware that assisting in a fraud is grounds for disbarment."

"That is an outrage!"

"The same goes for an attorney who knowingly presents false evidence."

"Get out!"

"Consider yourself served, Harvey. If you and your client decide to go through with this charade, I will take it to the ends of the earth. And I will personally see you never practice law again."

Brody knew something was seriously troubling Rae, just as he was certain she would not tell him what it was. He paced around the wintry lawn fronting his cottage, wishing he could do something to help her out, something worthwhile with his afternoon hours, something . . .

He walked around to the bookstore. When he stepped inside, the heavyset woman behind the counter gave him a slow up-and-down, then said, "Don't you dare claim to be here looking for a book."

"Actually, no. I was hoping for some advice."

"Is that all." Another of those slow looks. "You're the Reames fellow back in Cabin Eight."

"Six."

"Just so I know where to tell the single ladies to go knocking. What kind of advice were you after?"

Brody ignored the smiling faces that emerged from the shelves. "Emma doesn't have a Christmas tree."

"On account of how she ordered us all not to make her one."

He pointed hard in the direction of the back. "I was thinking I'd decorate the dogwoods and magnolias outside her bedroom window."

The woman's look changed. "Do you know, that's actually the sweetest thing I've heard all day."

"Can you tell me where I'd be able to buy some lights?"

"Three days before Christmas? Hmph. New York, maybe. Or Hong Kong. Not anyplace around here, that's for sure."

"What about ornaments, or something—"

"Hang on now, let me think." She inspected him a moment longer, then reached for her phone and tapped in a number, all without taking her eyes off Brody. "Hon, whatcha doing? Well, just record the game and come over here. I need . . . Okay, here's a news flash. Your shouting at the television ain't gonna make any difference to whether Carolina wins the bowl game. Hurry, now, this is important."

When she cut the connection, Brodie started, "Thank you so—"

"Hush now, I'm still in thinking mode."

An elderly gentleman stepped from the rear stacks and said, "Paster Long might be able to help."

"George, I believe I just saw that mental bulb of yours give off a dim glow."

He grinned and resumed searching the shelves. "These days that takes some doing."

"Reames, you know where the Community Church is at?"

"Sure. And it's Brody."

"I'm Marilee Baker." She was already tapping in another number. "Why don't you head on over and ask for Jonathan Long? If he can't help you, he'll know who can."

The drive took him past the town's main supermarket and hardware store. Brody stopped long enough to buy boat supplies in the form of a coffee maker, filters, ground coffee, and a case of bottled water. Then he went back a second time for disposable plates, cups, cutlery, and garbage bags. The Community Church formed a trio of buildings out past sports fields shared by the high school and junior high. When Brody pulled into the lot, he found a tall gangly man in his forties piling boxes of Christmas ornaments by the side entrance. "You Reames?"

"Brody."

"Jonathan." He shook hands. "How's Emma faring these days?"

"She wants to go sailing tomorrow."

"That's about the best news I've heard this season." He indicated the boxes. "I have no idea why we wind up with all this stuff. I keep telling people our back rooms can't be used for storage. But every year they drop off more stuff. Come on inside and see for yourself."

The activity hall was connected to the main church by a long air-conditioned passage, an absolute necessity during the stormy seasons. Three cavernous storerooms extended off one side. The central room was crammed with what appeared to be an army of Christmas elves, reindeers, and smiling Santas. Jonathan pointed to cartons stacked by the side wall. "All those hold lights. No idea if any of them still work."

"This is amazing."

"Every few years we put up a nativity scene—that's the gear under the canvas tarps at the back. You're welcome to take that as well, if you dare."

"Nix on the nativity," Brody replied. "I can pretty much imagine what Emma would say, having Joseph and Mary and the Three Wise Men staring through her bedroom window."

"We've got some extension cords around here somewhere." The pastor started away. "Why don't you load up what you want, I'll go see if I can find them."

In the end, Brody took everything except the manger scene.

When he returned with the fourth truckload, Brody found Marilee, her husband, three other women Brody didn't recognize, the elderly gentleman, and half a dozen student-age helpers stringing lights and erecting a Christmas scene in Emma's lawn. They were yelling at each other in whispers, waving arms, pointing at various empty spots, and generally having a grand time. Marilee greeted him with, "Emma was kind of asleep, so I went in and closed her curtains before we started this jamboree."

"Sort of asleep," Brody repeated.

"She came awake long enough to tell me closing the curtains at sundown was a first sign of dementia." Marilee's smile split her face in two. "I swear, that woman does love to moan."

Brody took his time unloading the final truckload. Sunset highlighted the trees rimming Emma's lawn. The single magnolia was so burnished by the late afternoon light it looked like painted porcelain. The wind had gentled to nearly nothing, faint puffs now veering slowly to the south. The temperature was dropping, but Brody was fairly certain the next morning would soon warm nicely.

Marilee directed the crew, a job she clearly relished. Brody helped steady a ladder as two students strung lights from higher branches. Then Olivia bounded into the garden with Mia and Cameron in tow. His sister hugged him and demanded, "This was all your idea? Really?"

"It sort of sprang from small beginnings."

Olivia embraced him more tightly still, then let their mother take her place. Mia inspected him carefully, then asked, "You've already gone to see your father?" When he nodded confirmation, she demanded, "How did it go?"

"Better than I could have ever hoped." He decided on the spot to tell both ladies, "We're taking Emma for a sail tomorrow. Would you like to come?"

"Can't," Olivia said. "We're driving to the in-laws for an early Christmas stuffing."

Mia asked, "You're sure there is room for one more?"

"Mom, the boat is forty-five feet. Yes, there's room." To Cameron, "You're more than welcome to join us."

She patted her stomach. "This is as far from home as I'm allowed these days."

"I'd love to come," Mia said. "Whose boat is it?"

"Mine, if I take a new job." Brody took a big breath. "And quit racing."

"Son, really?"

"It's all early days. But this is one option."

Olivia demanded, "Since when?"

"The new offer arrived two hours ago."

Olivia pretended to be cross. "You're keeping me from getting all red in the face and shouting at you for holding back. Again."

"That's the idea."

Which was good for a third hug. "Look who's growing up."

Marilee called over, "Mind you don't damage those goods. I've pretty much decided I'm going to plant my brand on this one."

Her husband snorted. "Am I supposed to pretend I didn't hear that?"

Marilee winked at Mia. "Pretend all you like, hon."

Brody fell into step with Cameron, who smiled at

him and said, "Don't mind me. I'll just waddle around a bit." She moved slowly, one hand on the small of her back. "I never understood the meaning of swollen until now."

He brought a rocking chair from his cottage porch and helped her settle. "I've been thinking a lot about our latest conversation, trying to understand the meaning of home."

"And?"

Brody waved toward the people, the joy. "Being part of this moment is as close as I've ever come."

She stroked her middle, a slow thoughtful motion. "Attachment theory plays a major role in the sort of transition you are experiencing. It happens when you can accept that you are truly safe, when you've established a secure base. This means you can be confident these elements will be part of your tomorrow. You see life and people and circumstances from a new perspective. You can be flexible. Take chances. Learn new things."

Brody was still mulling that over when his phone rang. He checked the screen and saw his old boss was the caller.

He stepped away. "Excuse me, I need to take this."

"Brody."

He turned back to find Cameron smiling. A first in this new lifetime. "It's nice to see you making such progress."

"Thanks."

She wasn't finished. "Nicer still to play a part in this transition."

"I may have spoken out of turn. You and your lady caught me off guard." Jacob Whitinger cleared his throat, again, a third time. Then, "I'm the one placing this call. Not some minion in legal or HR. Making amends. Trying to, anyway."

Brody walked away from the people and the Christmas cheer. None of it meshed with what he was hearing. He could imagine the arguments Jacob and his HR minions had been through, coming up with something this close to an apology, probably the first Jacob had made in years. "I understand."

"There's no way you're getting everything you want. That's not how the world turns. So here's what I'm offering."

His phone chimed with an incoming text. Brody put Jacob on speaker, drew up the text, and saw it was from Rae: She was on her way over, but had been forced to stop because the Atlanta firm's CEO had called and upgraded his offer with the requested signing bonus.

Shepphard Creighton was, as Rae put it, talking Christmas turkey.

Jacob continued laying out his own terms. As he did, Brody's phone chimed a second time. Rae's new text further outlined Creighton's offer. Brody stood and did his best to accept how two major groups were vying for his services at the very same time.

Three of the women and a couple of students chose that moment to start singing. The tune was "All I Want for Christmas." They were, in Brody's opinion, quite good.

Jacob felt otherwise. "What is all that racket?"

Brody replied, "Christmas."

20

Brody was in his pickup's rear hold, clearing the remnants from five loads of Christmas gear, when Rae walked around the home's front edge. She was texting and not really watching where she was going, just heading for his cottage, moving by rote.

Then she looked up and froze. Her look of utter confusion drew smiles from almost everyone, including Brody. He watched as her shoulders hunched slightly and her eyes went round, a little girl again, at least for this one moment, captured by a Christmas surprise.

Olivia walked over, patted her arm, said, "My brother made this happen."

She found him then, standing apart from the others, smiling. Then she rushed over and flung herself into Brody's arms.

Olivia offered a soft, "What do you know."

Marilee said, "I guess that means Santa didn't get my note."

Her husband told the others, "See what I have to put up with?"

Rae asked, "You really did this?"

"It was sort of my idea, yeah." Brody felt her nuzzle more tightly still, and knew all the others watched, and didn't care. As he pressed his face into the abundance of her hair and her scent, and held her gently, he decided this one incredible moment defined complete.

Rae released him only to take Brody's hand and guide him over to the cottage porch. There was only one rocker, since he had carried the other out for Cameron to use. Brody settled on the floor, close enough for Rae to reach him, if she wanted—which, apparently, she did. "Okay, so me flinging myself into your arms like that probably wasn't the most professional act of my young career."

Her hand rested on his shoulder, up close to his collar so she could stroke his hairline. He remained silent until she used one fingernail to poke his bare neck. A silent demand for him to speak. Brody told her exactly what he had been thinking, which was, "You are without a doubt the most passionate woman I have ever known."

The motions of her fingers slowed, the hand withdrew, her legs lifted so that her feet touched the chair, and she wrapped her arms around her shins. "So many people think I'm cold."

"Then they don't know you."

"Analytical. Domineering."

"Okay, sure, being a good attorney is one of your passions. So, yes. When you're working, you are all of those things. Along with diligent. Incredibly intelligent. Dedicated. Fiercely loyal." He stopped and searched for more, but all he could come up with was, "It means so much to know you, at least a little. I trust you with my life."

He couldn't believe he'd actually spoken those words. From Rae's silence, she apparently thought the same.

Then Marilee and Olivia walked over, their smiles a gentle approval. Olivia said, "Emma's awake."

They trundled through the bookstore, all seventeen of them, grinning and whispering, Cameron hissing for quiet from her place in back. When they entered the hall, Emma was up and standing in the kitchen doorway. She demanded, "What on earth?"

Rae stepped forward. "You just come with us."

"But I'm hungry."

"We'll get you anything you like in a minute." She pried Emma's hands free of the walker. "What are you in the mood for?"

"Privacy would do me just fine, thank you very much."

"Coming right up." Rae guided Emma around and headed for the kitchen door. "Brody, give me a hand with the old bat."

Together they steadied her through the rear door, onto the porch, and over to where a trio of smiling reindeer flanked her rear steps. Marilee called over to where her husband stood holding the extension leads. "All right, Harry. Let 'er rip."

The lights came on all at once.

The trees were linked now, forming an illuminated and blinking wall. The central magnolia was ablaze with color, and crowned with a brightly shining star.

Brody thought Emma looked frail as spun crystal. The colorful glow only heightened her fragility. He could see the trembling effort required to keep herself upright, even with their help. So he moved closer still, just in case. Which meant he was there to observe a tear trickle down the side of her face.

Emma declared, "Great heavens above."

Brody realized Rae was also shedding tears. "Merry Christmas, Emma."

"Child, this is the gaudiest monstrosity I've ever laid eyes on." She hugged Rae closer. "And you are the dearest, sweetest angel on this entire earth."

21

The next morning, Brody was up with the dawn. While his coffee brewed, he checked the online charts—tides and weather and winds and currents. Forecasts for ocean sailors extended out over several hundred miles, some as far south as the Venezuelan coast. Today he restricted himself to the region beyond the Shackleford Banks. He thought they would head out to Cape Lookout, maybe as far as the northern tip of Cedar Island if Emma was up to it. He drank coffee on the cottage's stubby porch, gauging the wind and weather for himself. He decided it would indeed be a fine day, and set out.

He stopped by the same taqueria, where construction workers and delivery drivers stood in sleepy silence drinking strong Mexican coffee. He followed a long-held habit and ordered a dozen breakfast burritos. He ate one of the thin flour tortillas filled with eggs and sharp cheese and chorizo and cilantro as he crossed the island bridge.

When he pulled into the marina parking lot, the office was still closed, the docks silent. He unlocked the vessel, entered the galley, placed the burritos in the warming oven, and set the temperature on low. Then he brewed fresh coffee, poured himself a mug, and returned topside.

Brody had no idea how the day would pan out. There was a very real possibility that sailing minus the tight discipline, the adrenaline rush of competition, the heady joy of a big win, wouldn't hold him. But he didn't think so. Watching the day take shape, Brody caught flashes of something so potent he feared it might be forbidden. As if a joy this strong could never be his. As if the closest he could ever come to true contentment was to glimpse it in the faces of others.

But he heard whispers of a new melody, one suggesting he had indeed started the necessary turning. That here in this wintry dawn was the chance of a new life's course.

"What does a girl have to do to get a coffee around here?"

Rae was dressed in a navy turtleneck and matching slicker. Pale denim slacks, slip-on boat shoes. Canvas satchel slung from one shoulder. Her hair was partially tucked inside his extra knit cap, the one from his glove box that she had apparently kept. Brody thought she had never looked lovelier. "Where's Emma?"

"Amiya and your mother are bringing her."

"Great. Who's Amiya?"

"The friend I told you about yesterday, remember?"

He had a vague recollection of something mentioned in the whirlwind of events, but what really held him was Rae's somber expression. "Welcome aboard, sailor."

He stowed her gear belowdecks and returned with a second mug to find Rae had taken position in the skipper's chair. She accepted the coffee, then snagged his hand, keeping him close. Rae examined him with those astonishing aquamarine eyes, unblinking in their intensity. "We need to talk."

Those softly spoken four words were enough for his heart to start thumping like a great kettledrum, *boom-boom-boom*. He set his mug on the transom and realized his entire body was now caught by subtle tremors.

Rae told him, "When we were together before, the last thing I worried about, the very last, was you breaking my heart. There wasn't any risk of that, because it was already shattered. You helped fill an empty void. You gave me a reason to smile again. Without you, I don't know how I might have found

my way back." She sipped her mug without taking
her eyes off him. "Now is very, very different."

Another pause, another sip. Brody felt as if time
had flowed away, an unseen current that no longer
touched them. This craft was now held in the grip of
a woman's gaze and softly spoken words, so powerful
it could set a compass heading unique to them and
this gathering day.

Rae continued, "All I've gained from my string of
broken romances is a clear idea of what I really want.
A love strong enough to hold both our private and
our professional worlds. So potent we can be our-
selves and walk different paths yet know we walk
them together. A life we live in unity, happy in our
times apart, connected wherever our work and re-
sponsibilities go. Talking and sharing whatever we
face . . ."

She paused midsentence and gave a slow and
thoughtful nod. Brody had the sense of her reflecting on what she had said and deciding it was enough.
Either he was able to finish the sentence for them
both or not. Her unblinking intensity stripped him
bare. Which was absolutely necessary. A vital component of this moment beyond time's reach.

He began, "I've never known the meaning of the
word *relationship*. I've been too blind to see beyond
the momentary and too wounded to give back. I've
basically kept everything about myself a secret,

walled off from everyone. I took whatever was offered, gave nothing, and hurt a lot of people in the process."

Despite his yammering heart and unsteady voice, Brody saw the day with utmost clarity. As if being honest with a good woman lifted the veil from his eyes. And what he saw . . .

Her solemn and open gaze granted him the strength to continue: "I've loved you from the first moment you stepped on the marina's front deck. I knew you were brokenhearted and couldn't give me more than a few days or weeks. It wasn't enough, but I knew it was more than I deserved. So, I did what I could to be the man you needed. Day after day I watched you knit your world back together. Until you were ready to leave me. I wanted to spare you that, too. So I lied. The only lie I've ever told you. I said we were starting ocean trials. And we were. But not for another month. So, we parted and my heart was broken for the first and only time. And I went back to my string of fake romances. Until last spring, when one day it all just fell apart. I decided it was time to stop living the lies. I didn't have a clue what truth was, or what I should do now with all this empty space in my life. But that was the turning point. . . ."

Brody stopped because the words were no longer there. Just one thought remained. One simple truth he had to reveal, no matter how great the risk. "I have no idea what true love is. Or how to forge a real relationship. I know how to pretend. But that time of my life is over. I never want to do that, not ever again, not for as long as I live. I want to learn, Rae. But you'll have to teach me. Show me how—"

That was as far as she let him go.

22

They were still locked in an embrace when a dark Mercedes van pulled up to the marina entrance. Brody slowly pulled away far enough to trace one finger along the contours of Rae's face. He was mesmerized by how the rising sun formed prisms in her gaze. Then he spotted his mother slipping from the van's rear hold. "They're here." As they untangled, Brody added, "Thank you, Rae."

Her smile was gentle now. Tender. "You don't need to thank me."

"Yes, I do. Every day."

Brody followed Rae up the pier, marveling at how everything about the morning remained as it had been an hour earlier. Same daylight, same southerly wind, same gulls and sounds and smells. Yet utterly new, polished to a shimmering hue that filled him with a fizzing joy.

A stunningly beautiful woman with caramel skin

and liquid dark gaze rose from the van. She smiled at Rae's approach, accepted her embrace, and all the while she studied Brody. She spoke too softly for the words to carry, and something Rae said in response caused her to squeal with delight. They embraced a second time, and the woman flashed another look at Brody. Not so much worried as cautious. Inspecting him down to the level of bone and sinew, all in three seconds flat.

The van's driver was an older gentleman who carried himself with a stiffly formal air. Brody walked around to the van's other side as the gentleman slid open the rear door, touched a button, and watched as a ramp slid smoothly out. He reached inside, unhooked clamps, and wheeled Emma's chair into the sunlight.

"Hello, dear boy." She accepted his embrace, then waved in the gentleman's direction. "Say hello to Jiyan, my new best friend. I'm still trying to figure out how I survived this long without him and this wonderful ride."

The gentleman revealed the ability to smile warmly while remaining formal. "I am at your beck and call, madame."

"Promises, promises."

Jiyan offered Brody his hand. "This lady thinks the world of you, Mr. Reames."

"Brody."

He nodded with his entire upper body. Then the smile returned as he said, "Day or night, Ms. Alden. Day or night."

Brody wheeled her chair around the van and started down the ramp. Emma demanded, "What are those three chattering about?"

"Me, most likely."

She sniffed. "Well, they can do it on the boat." She looked back to where the driver followed, arms full of packages and quilts. "Jiyan, would you kindly help this young man wrestle me on board?"

"No wrestling," Brody said. "Not on my boat."

They lashed Emma's chair into position by the rear gunnel, granting her a wide-open view. The craft was equipped with a Volvo diesel that purred like a contented cat. When Brody invited the gentleman to join them, Amiya responded, "Jiyan, don't you dare." To the others, she explained, "Jiyan has promised to spy on Daddy and Curtis for me."

"I have done no such thing and never would."

Emma told the young woman, "You still haven't explained why you're one and not three."

"Daddy woke up feeling poorly, or so he claims." Amiya sniffed her disapproval. "Curtis arrived last night. He says he's tired."

Jiyan offered, "Curtis is just back from Delhi. Where he met with the board. He says the journey was a battle from start to finish."

Amiya rolled her eyes. "He's young. He could have rested on the boat." To the others, "Curtis wants a day with Daddy. Alone."

"That much is correct," Jiyan said.

"How the two of them will accomplish anything without my input is a mystery for the ages," Amiya said.

Jiyan bowed to Emma. "Have a lovely trip."

Amiya said, "You men will miss me terribly."

"A day of peace and quiet and male company." Jiyan stepped onto the dock. "Heaven."

Even this deep in winter, the southerly wind carried a silken melody. Brody set aside his outer gear as he motored them from the marina, glad the ladies were busy with Emma. He needed his own moment to gauge how it felt, heading into open waters, with no hint of a coming race. The boat was remarkably responsive, even now while under motor. He joined the early morning traffic, most of them headed for the wind-sheltered beaches of Shackleford Point. Amiya's supplies included two picnic hampers and a mound of quilts. Brody watched as she settled one around Emma, who naturally complained the entire time. Amiya finally had enough of that and huffed her way into the cabin, where Rae and his mother were brewing fresh coffee and preparing the burritos.

Emma called to Amiya's retreat, "I'm not a child, you know."

Brody kept his back to the lady and her chair. "I hope you're not talking to me, because I'm not listening."

A silence, then: "I suppose I can wait and spank you once we're in open waters."

When Amiya returned topside, she told Emma, "I've laid out a nice pallet for when you grow tired of being a nasty, cantankerous old fussbudget."

Emma replied, "One day soon you'll be covered in wrinkles and warts and all your fine hair will fall out."

Amiya stuck out her tongue and retreated to the galley.

Brody glanced at Emma and said quietly, "I don't think Amiya likes me."

"She's worried, is all." Emma also kept her voice low, so her words did not carry into the galley. "Amiya cared for Rae when events left her wounded and alone."

The wind freshened as they approached Shackleford Point. Blackbeard had once moored his vessels in those sheltered waters. A century later, whalers built a working harbor village. Now the islands formed part of a wildlife preserve. Brody's craft had electric winches, allowing a lone sailor to maintain control of the helm while adjusting the sails. Once they were beyond the crowd of pleasure craft, he decided it was time to go sailing. Brody watched carefully as the sails rose for the first time. Another set of controls allowed him to draw in the sheets and halt the luffing. That done, he cut the motor. The soft cymbals of waves tapping his hull, the hum of wind through the halyards, became the day's dominant melody.

The wind gusted, a larger wave struck the gunnel, and water splashed over the side. Brody kept a one-handed grip on the wheel as he turned and said, "We can hold to the inland waterway and sail the Back Sound."

"Don't you dare."

"It could get rough," he warned.

"Does it appear to you that I'm the least bit concerned?" Emma's face shone despite the droplets. "Sail on, young man."

He set the autopilot long enough to drape his slicker over her like a blanket. He pulled the cap off his own head and settled it on Emma. "Now you look the part."

After they passed the Shackleford Pockets, Brody turned east by north, taking aim for Lookout Bight. The boat lacked a racer's stallionlike sensitivity. But it also did not need the nonstop care and minute attention required to hold a racer on course. This was a hybrid, meant both for racing and family outings. Emma hummed the occasional note, pausing only to smile and pat Amiya's cheek when she emerged with steaming mugs and burritos wrapped in linen napkins. Rae joined him by the wheel, and together they ate and swayed to the ocean's dance. All the sensations came together for Brody then, a musical whisper of emotions and timeless joy so intense, he allowed the wind and sun to pluck a tear from his eye. Another.

His mother and Amiya settled in the bow, where a shallow indentation formed a cushioned pocket mostly free from the wind. Amiya chattered happily while his mother smiled and occasionally sent Brody a warm glance. It was just like Mia, the woman happiest when silent and aware and listening. Rae formed a welcome and warming presence beside him, until Emma called, "Dear, would you mind if I had a private word with your beau?"

Brody waited for her to contradict the older woman, claim the word did not apply, not yet. Something. Instead, Rae merely smiled at him and said, "You're called aft. Did I say that right?"

He wanted to laugh, sing, kiss her. "Think you're ready to take the helm?"

"Point and shoot, right?"

He tapped the console's oversize compass. "Hold to this heading."

"Aye-aye, Skipper. Your word is my something or other. At least for now."

Which was good for a kiss. When Brody settled on the bench beside Emma, he expected her to comment about the smooch, his goofy grin, them together. Instead, she said, "You're talking with Cameron."

Brody liked how she framed it. Making a statement, not asking a question. Emma was clearly fine with him brushing the words aside and shutting that door. Instead, he replied, "She's helping me. A lot."

"I'm glad." Emma made a subtle shift and a wince, but when he reached out, she waved his hands away. "What are you two talking about?"

"Right now, we're focused on the meaning of home."

"That's a big one, sure enough." A silence, then, "Are you open to an old woman's opinion?"

"You've helped shape my world since I was a kid," he replied, glad for the chance to say those words. "Opine away."

"I've always seen love as a place. You work and you build and you hope, and all of a sudden, this new place appears in your mind and heart. And your world. That most of all." She studied Rae standing by the wheel, swaying in time to the ocean's rhythm. "You can dwell in it, find shelter and comfort in the hard times. Brease easy, find joy, somewhere to grow and thrive."

Brody rocked in time to the boat's motions. "Home."

23

The Shackleford Banks was a narrow strip of sand and coastal vegetation that extended from the Beaufort Inlet to Cape Lookout. The island's easternmost point almost connected with the next island, known as Core Banks. The southern tip of Core Banks formed a sharpish elbow, one that framed Shackleford on three sides, forming the deepwater cove known as Lookout Bay.

Brody sailed them through the Bardon Inlet cut, then lowered the sails and motored them into the sheltered cove. Rae feared the curving beaches that fronted the inland waterway would be jammed with holiday boats, but today was their gift. A trio of motorized craft were anchored out past Catfish Point, but otherwise the inlet was empty, the waters a deep wintry azure.

Somewhere during the voyage, an idea had taken

hold, strong as the day and the wind. Stronger. When
sea oats and windswept pines formed a filigree against
the morning sun, Rae knew with utter certainty how
her day was going to unfold.

She breathed the sharp sea-scented air and waited
impatiently as Brody drew them slowly shoreward.
When the sandy bottom became visible, he cut the engine and slipped into the waist-deep frigid waters.
Once Rae handed him the boat's anchors he slung
them over his shoulders and waded toward the beach.
Brody then returned to the craft's leeward side and
held out his arms. "Beachside taxi service. Today
only, special price."

As if in response, there was a soft splash off the
boat's stern. Amiya soon appeared, pushing through
the waters beyond the bow.

Brody asked, "Was it something I said?"

"Give it time." Mia reached down and allowed
Brody to take hold. When she was comfortably set in
a fireman's carry, she went on, "She's just being protective of Rae."

When it was Rae's turn, Brody started toward where
Amiya stood with his mother. A trio of dunes curved
with the island, forming a natural barrier against the
wind. Rae tapped his shoulder and pointed them toward a solitary stretch further north. The island flat-

tened here, allowing easy passage to the other side. But it also funneled the wind. Even as they approached the shore, Rae could feel the wintry bite.

There were so many things she wanted to tell Brody. She knew he was troubled by Amiya's silent wariness. He needed to be reassured. But just then the pressure to knit the day together with the past clogged Rae's throat so tight she could scarcely breathe. Soon as the water was ankle-deep, she wriggled free of his grasp and bolted. Rae heard Brody call after her and then Mia telling her son to let her go, give her space. All that only made her run faster. Rae had to do this while there was still time.

The cloudless sky was a deep blue-black, the light clear and intense. The saddle ended where the island met the ocean. The beach was different here, the sand coarser and so deep she sunk to midcalf with each step.

She searched.

As she did, the memories crowded in. Rae did not resist the onslaught. This was why she came, alone and bereft. This long-denied wound needed to be exposed and cleansed.

She recalled that terrible teenage Christmas. Growing into a new season of life, and shattered by all the losses she had been forced to endure. Both parents, home, the security she had taken for granted. Living now with Emma, who even then was partially crippled by arthritis. Rae had discovered the power of screaming at the top of her lungs, filled with a rage so potent she had no alternative but to let it out. Pouring wrath at the woman who had given this orphan a home.

Rae had no idea how long she remained in that dreadful state. Weeks. Then on this very day, the morning before Christmas Eve, Emma had borrowed a motorboat from Travis, Brody's uncle. Rae had loved the water since birth. Much as she wanted to refuse, Rae had come along for the ride. But she had remained isolated in the craft's bow, separated by all possible distance from her aunt.

Emma had brought them here. To Lookout Bay. Soon as they were moored on the beach, she told Rae the secret of sea glass. How years of hardship and grinding forces and solitary turmoil fashioned those simple elements into nature's finest gemstones.

She then told Rae they were staying here long as it took for Rae to find her an ocean jewel. One that marked the end of Rae's transition to womanhood.

Of course, Rae had never thought of her rage in those terms. And hearing Emma call it that had stripped her bare. Silenced her. Sent her ashore and running through this very same saddle to the oceanside beach. Where she stood in the biting winter wind, under a crystal blue-black sky. When it all came crashing down.

Great torrents of fury and remorse and sorrow

flooded through her, strong as the waves she could no longer see. Rae stood at the shoreline and felt her life collapse and re-form, wave after wave, like this was the story of her life, to be repeated endlessly in her island world beside the sunlit sea.

She started her search.

She found six gemstones, all different shapes and sizes. Two were ruby red, one smoky whitish gray, three in shades of blue. The final piece was a rarity, a blue paler than the winter sky and large as her thumb. Rae held it up, fascinated by how the tiny bubbles imbedded in the glass formed a series of circular prisms. They caught the light and spun it in magical precision.

Rae had hardly known she had fallen to her knees until the frigid water lapped against her thighs. She wept, only now there was an almost beautiful quality to her sorrow.

She remained where she was, long after the tears were finished, until her entire lower body was drenched by the incoming tide. Rae felt bonded to the waves and the day and the transition, a kinship so intense she didn't want to let the moment go. But the chill finally settled into her bones, so she rose and walked back, clutching her treasures with both hands.

When Rae returned to the little craft, Emma welcomed her with towels and blankets and a thermos of hot cocoa and a long tender embrace.

They had held onto each other that entire journey home.

"Rae?"

She turned around, but all she saw were prisms. One silhouette moved closer. She realized it was Brody. "You followed me."

"I wanted make sure you were all right."

"I need to find Emma a sea glass. For Christmas." She looked down, but everything was just a blur. "It's so hard."

She felt him step closer still, the sand grinding softly beneath his bare feet. But he did not touch her. Instead, he just remained there, in case she needed him.

Which she did. Desperately.

He said, "Can we look together?"

But his words only planted her more firmly in place. Immobile. "I feel like all my hope has drained away."

He shifted so close his shadow blocked the light. "Rae . . ."

"What?"

"You've given me so much. And part of this is learning to trust that hope is real."

She felt a tear slide down the tip of her nose and drop onto the sand. Wanting to wipe it away. But just then it was too much. "I'm so worried about Emma."

Now he touched her. One hand on the nape of her

neck, sliding under her hair and resting on her bare skin. Gentle as his voice. "We'll care for her best we can, for as long as we have."

She nodded, dislodging more tears.

"It's not enough and it never will be. But it's all we have." He waited with her then, patient. Watchful. There.

"Thank you, Brody."

"What was it you told me back on the boat? Something about never needing to speak those words?" His other hand reached for hers. "Come on, let's find Emma's gift."

24

They came back through the Shackleford cut just as the sun touched the western tree line. Coppery hues spread across the inland waters, forming a wintry farewell to their voyage.

The wind shifted north and sharpened. Emma woke from her nap in the galley and wanted to return on deck. Before moving her, Brody took all of Amiya's quilts and surrounded her with a rainbow nest. Emma complained, "I'm boiling."

"Not for long you're not."

"You've buried me in fourteen layers. I must look a sight."

Rae stood by the galley sink, across from Emma's perch. Amiya was positioned in the bow, watchful and silent. Rae confirmed, "Like a plump Persian doll."

Brody squatted down and slipped his arms under her. "Ready?"

"Give me a moment so I can swat that smart-mouthed young lady like she deserves."

"Arm around my neck. Here we go."

He made a careful shift up the five narrow steps and emerged into the increasingly frigid air. Mia watched from the helmsman's station, smiling approval. Brody used his chin to point at the stern bench. "Would you like to travel home from back there?"

"Child, you can take me anywhere you like."

"You'll be fully exposed to the wind," Brody explained. "Thus, all the covers."

She smiled approval as Brody gently settled her. "You really are a dear sweet man."

Rae waited until Brody stepped back, then tucked the quilts up around her. "Why don't you ever speak to me like that?"

"I do," she replied. "All the time. You're just not listening."

Amiya emerged a few moments later with mugs of hot cocoa. She handed one to Brody without meeting his gaze. She watched as Rae moved in close and slipped her arm around Brody's waist. Amiya then returned to the cushioned bow alcove, partially sheltered from the wind.

Brody's mother left her perch beside Emma. As she passed her son, Mia said, "Give her time."

He watched Amiya and Mia settle on cushions, comfortable as cats in the coppery sun. Brody decided

Rae's silent presence bonded to his side was all the assurance he needed, at least for just then.

As they passed the first buoy marker, Rae said, "A doubloon for your thoughts."

"Right then, at that very moment, I was wondering what makes you so happy about practicing law."

She remained silent until they entered the main channel. Then she released him and swung around, taking up station by the controls. "Sometimes I lay awake at night, astonished by how fortunate I am to be a small-town lawyer on my own. It's allowed me to remain what I've always been, a practical idealist." The wind tossed her hair about, a dark and tangled forest now framing her face. If Rae even noticed she gave no sign. "It's been said that the practice of law is nothing more than the application of arcane rules to an uncooperative reality. And on the bad days, I think that's being far too complimentary. Laws remain just dead words on a page. There to be twisted and corrupted by cynics and cheats."

The setting sun flashed golden among her tresses, flickering and dancing. All he could clearly see now were her eyes. "And the good days?"

"When it works as it should, the law is a living, breathing entity. All people of this great and wonderful nation are treated equally, regardless of title or power or wealth. The rule of law demands nothing less."

"Rae . . ."

"What?"

But the words just didn't come.

Just the same, she must have found what she wanted, for she slipped back around and kissed him soundly. When Brody opened his eyes again, his mother smiled. Amiya watched, her gaze hooded. Concerned.

As they rounded Bogue Banks, Brody started the engine and asked Rae to take the helm. He then hit the switches and moved forward to ensure the winches drew both sails in smoothly. He felt both weary and content. The day had left him sated in ways he would never have thought possible. As he lashed the jib and mainsail's boom into place, he thought of what Emma had said about home. The place he had never found for himself. Until now.

Amiya chose that moment to turn and inspect him, clearly uncertain who he was, or what role he really was meant to play. At some bone-deep level, Brody agreed with her. He started back, gripped by that uncertainty, fearing it was all a monumental mistake. The sun would fully set, and when night stretched out its starlit wings, these wonderful people would all come fully awake. And his fable of having found love and a home would evaporate. It was almost more than he could bear.

He tried to slip past Rae, step down into the cabin,

find a dark corner. And do what he had his whole life long. Hide.

"Brody." Rae snagged his arm.

Turning around, not shrugging off her hand, was a terrible ordeal. It went against years of ingrained habit. But he did so, and saw that Emma's eyes were open and watchful and burning like sunset coals.

Rae said, "Tell me what's the matter."

He shifted around and moved in closer, so her hair shielded his face. "What you said earlier," he managed. "I don't think I can survive a broken heart."

She shifted back a trace, far enough to hold his gaze. "You're afraid."

He nodded.

"So am I. Terrified. But I still think what we're doing is right. Do you?"

His nod grew until it took hold of his entire frame. "I want to be good for you, Rae."

"Shall I tell you what to do?"

"Please. Now. Always."

The hand holding his arm pulled him around. "Move in behind me. No, closer. That's it. So we touch from feet to hairline. Okay, reach around me, nestle me in your arms. Good. That's it, reach out and hold the wheel." She drew in closer still. "Now take us home."

25

It was almost fully dark when they moored quayside. Amiya's limo-van waited by the main buildings. Charlie Trafford, the marina's general manager, stood on the waterfront deck talking with a couple dressed in Palm Beach casual. He sketched a wave in Brody's general direction, then drew the couple inside.

Brody and Rae made the boat ready to leave overnight while Amiya and his mother carried the remnants of the day's meal and the wheelchair to where Jiyan waited. Brody locked up the cabin, then went back to where Rae squatted beside the slumbering Emma. He slid his arms under the older woman and scooped her up, still encased in Amiya's multicolored quilts. The woman seemed weightless. Rae walked alongside, holding Emma's hand.

The ever solemn driver stayed well clear as Brody settled Emma on the van's rear seat. Brody then watched as Rae took his place and strapped Emma in. Amiya stepped up beside him and asked, "You will follow us?"

They were the first words she had spoken directly to him all day.

Rae emerged from the van and replied for him. "We'll be right behind you."

They drove in comfortable silence and made good time. As they crossed the Radio Island bridge, music drifted through their open windows. Brody slowed with all the other traffic and watched the traditional Christmas boat parade exit the Beaufort marina. Lights were strung everywhere imaginable, blinking and adding to the semi-chaotic good cheer. The festive crowd lining the Beaufort waterfront greeted the parade with cheers and sparklers and honking horns.

Brody continued on. The celebration did not lure him as it often had in the past. Theirs was a different season, or so it seemed.

Rae must have felt the same, for she squeezed his hand and said, "Next year."

Her words warmed him as much as anything in that long and monumental day.

When they parked in Emma's front drive, Brody and Rae took up the same positions, him carrying and her holding Emma's hand. Only this time Mia and the silent beauty followed close behind as they entered Emma's bedroom. Brody returned outside and waited with the silent Jiyan, watching the sky. The moon was almost full, flickering in and out of view as clouds pushed their way across the sky. The night smelled of coming rain.

When the ladies came out, Amiya was the first to approach him. Her eyes were dark lantern-glows as she studied him. "You and I will speak together soon, yes?"

Brody decided he liked this mystery woman just fine. "But not tonight."

She rewarded him with a brief smile and feather-light embrace. Jiyan had the front passenger door open, and she slid inside. Jiyan walked around to the driver's door and closed it behind him. Now it was just Rae and his mother.

Mia smiled in a manner as warm and silken as the night wind. "My patience and my prayers are finally answered."

Brody had no idea what to say, and remained silent.

She smiled at that as well. "Happy birthday, son."

Rae said, "I thought . . ."

"The hospital registered him as a Christmas Eve child," Mia said. But he came into this world three minutes before midnight."

Brody shrugged. "Today, tomorrow, none of that kept me from feeling cheated when it came to presents."

"And look at you now." Mia embraced him, then walked over and slipped into the van's rear hold.

When it was just the two of them, Rae held him. Brody was beyond glad she remained silent. The day was just too full for more words. She kissed him, and must have liked the flavor, because she kissed him a second time, then once more. She released him, stepped back, and murmured, "Tomorrow."

Brody remained standing there long after the van pulled away. It felt beyond right, experiencing a solitary end to this most magnificent of days. The distance he had journeyed between sunrise and now was so vast, he suspected one strong gust could sweep him away, carry him far from this mystical realm where Christmas wishes might indeed come true.

As he started back toward the darkened lawn ornaments, he thought the wind whispered his name. Then he heard it a second time, and realized Emma was calling.

When he reentered her bedroom, she asked, "Are they gone?"

"Yes." When she made feeble motions to sit up, he helped place additional pillows behind her back. "Better?"

"Much." She sat with eyes closed, breathing shallow puffs. The parchment stain was back to her features now. "We've had a good day."

"The best."

She cast her gaze about the room. "Where is the sea glass you and Rae found for me?"

"In my pocket."

She reached out. "May I?"

"Of course. They're yours."

"Thank you, Brody." She clasped the three pieces with both hands. "Maybe you should move my phone closer."

He set it by her water glass. "I could sleep here if you like."

She huffed, "Now you're talking Rae's kind of silliness."

"If you need anything . . ."

"I'll call. Don't worry." When he remained standing between her bed and the doorway, she turned sharpish. "Here's the point where a gentleman makes his exit."

26

Christmas Eve dawned gray and mysterious, a veiled sunrise that cast the world in a pewter glow. Brody shaved and dressed while the coffee brewed. When he passed the kitchen table on his way to the porch, Brody realized he had left his phone off all night.

"What a goof."

He opened his cottage door to be greeted by a puff of warm wind. The southerly storm had passed with the night, and now the clouds overhead were gradually breaking up.

As he stepped onto the porch, the veil parted and a blade of purest gold spilled down. Abruptly the entire rear garden was alive with sparkling prisms, every rainbow hue and more besides. Brody was mesmerized by the sight. He stood rimmed by a field of liquid gold.

He knew the moment was fleeting. The clouds

might bunch together again at any moment. Another southerly squall could push through, making it just another dismal gray winter day.

None of it mattered.

There before him, a new season was unfolding.

The last time he had known such unadulterated joy, Brody had viewed his island summer as never ending. Now he knew better.

This was a season of change and growth and challenge. And love. Yes, even for him.

Then his mother appeared on Emma's back porch. She waved to him, which proved an awkward movement, as her arms were filled with Amiya's quilts. She settled them one by one into a porch rocker as Emma appeared in the doorway behind her. Mia shook her head at Brody even before he started to move, holding him where he was. Brody watched her mother help Emma settle into the padded chair.

Once the older woman was down and comfortable, and encased in a final quilt, Mia walked over, embraced her son, wished him a Merry Christmas, and asked, "Is there more of that coffee?"

Brody poured her a mug and added too much milk and sugar, how she had always taken it. She sipped, nodded approval, and said, "You kept your phone off last night?"

"I forgot to turn it on."

"Probably just as well. You wouldn't have gotten much sleep otherwise." Mia's lustrous silver hair was drawn back and pinned firmly in place. "Rae is on her way over. Prepare to be scolded."

"I probably deserve it."

"Less than some, no more than most." Another sip. "Cameron went into labor just after midnight. Rae and Olivia and Amiya spent the night at the hospital. Cameron and her husband have a lovely baby girl."

"I'm glad." Brody felt the cottage's front room become filled with a long overdue remorse. All the wrong moves, the secrets, formed into a blanket cast over the season. "Mom—"

"Don't."

"I just want—"

"Brody, don't." When she was certain he would stay quiet, Mia continued, "If you allow, regret over wrong moves and imperfect actions can crush you. You must learn how to let go."

"I don't know how. Or if I can."

"Or if you actually deserve release, isn't that what you're thinking?" Her smile carried a timeless element. "I am your mother. Who better to say this is the Christmas gift you must grant yourself?"

Brody was halted from needing to respond by a cascade of blaring horns and happy voices and doors slamming and laughter. As they stepped onto the cottage porch, Rae spotted him and told the others, "Call off the dogs! He's alive!"

He was barely down the cottage steps before she rushed into his arms. Brody accepted her kiss, and said, "I can explain."

"It won't help. But don't worry. I'll be cross with you later." She grabbed his arm and pulled him forward. "Hi, Mia. Come watch."

People continued to stream around the house, Olivia and Amiya among them. A woman started singing "The Bells of Christmas Morn." Brody was enormously glad it wasn't Rae. The woman couldn't carry a tune in a trawler.

Rae had on the same clothes she'd worn on the boat. Her hair was matted and her eyes were red-rimmed. Brody asked, "Did you sleep?"

"Some. A little. Not much. And that was on a hospital bench." She tugged him forward. "Can you possibly move any slower?"

So he allowed himself to be dragged through the crowd that still kept growing. She didn't actually shove people aside. More like, she got in close enough for them to smile in her direction and step aside.

They maneuvered over to where Olivia knelt beside Emma's rocker. Brody's sister hit speed-dial, waited, then said, "We're here. Okay, just one second."

She lowered the phone, pressed a button, asked, "Can you see us?"

Cameron's voice replied, "Sure. Hi, everyone."

"Okay, here goes." Olivia's smile was wondrous to behold. She swung the phone around so the screen was pointed at the older woman. "Say hello to Cameron's baby girl. Her name is Emma."

Brody took in Emma's tremulous joy, then turned so as to watch the others. He did not so much see their smiles and tears and joy, as absorb. All the emotions, everything he was open to accept. He looked down at Rae, saw her brush the tears off her cheeks, and offered her a fierce embrace.

Home.